Undercover Nurse

Undercover Nurse

Jane Converse

G.K. Hall & Co. • Chivers Press
Waterville, Maine USA   Bath, England

This Large Print edition is published by G.K. Hall & Co., USA and by Chivers Press, England.

Published in 2002 in the U.S. by arrangement with Maureen Moran Agency.

Published in 2002 in the U.K. by arrangement with the author.

U.S. Softcover 0-7838-9732-4 (Paperback Series Edition)
U.K. Hardcover 0-7540-4800-4 (Chivers Large Print)

The text of this Large Print edition is unabridged.
Other aspects of the book may vary from the original edition.

Set in 16 pt. Plantin by Elena Picard.

Printed in the United States on permanent paper.

British Library Cataloguing-in-Publication Data available

Library of Congress Cataloging-in-Publication Data

Converse, Jane.
    Undercover nurse / Jane Converse.
        p. cm.
    ISBN 0-7838-9732-4 (lg. print : sc : alk. paper)
    1. Nurses — Fiction. 2. Large type books. I. Title.
PS3553.O544 U53 2002
    813′.54—dc21   2001051845

Undercover Nurse

One

Gail Arnold said good-bye to the shy fortyish man who was the last outpatient on the day's schedule and locked the dispensary door behind him. "Pete's gotten a raise. Did he tell you, Doctor? Automatic raise at the end of six months. He's so proud of himself."

Bruce Cranston finished recording the injection on the patient's chart. "That wouldn't sound impressive to anybody but an ex-junkie. For Pete, being on the same job, not having to hustle a hundred dollars a day to support his habit . . . wow! It's like a miracle. Sad thing is, the guy had quite a musical career going for him when he got hooked on heroin. Played jazz clarinet."

"Dr. Roper told me," Gail said. "I guess this was before our time."

"Right. But Roper claims Pete was becoming a name in his field." The doctor sighed, slipped the chart into its file folder, and got up from behind his desk. "Washing taxicabs. Quite a step down from being a recording star."

"And quite a step up," Gail reminded the young doctor. "I mean, from being driven to holding up cabdrivers to raise a hundred dollars each and every day. And then going through a cold-turkey withdrawal on the floor of a jail cell after he got caught. Pete gets cold chills just remembering that horror. And he's so grateful now, so amazed that the same cab company he used to steal from hired him."

Bruce nodded. "The owner happens to be an enlightened guy. Mr. Villanelle's one of the heaviest private contributors to the clinic. And he puts his heart where his money is. He knows you can't 'cure' a junkie. You can keep him off his habit with methadone, but you've got to give him a reason for staying off the junk. He knows most addicts have insecure personalities. Full of neuroses that drove them into the escape route in the first place. So, assuming the addict wants to get well, what happens to his determination, what happens to his self-respect if he's pegged as a 'dope fiend' and nobody wants to give him a job? Mr. Villanelle doesn't just serve on the clinic's board of supervisors or write a big tax-deductible check once a year, the way some of our other so-called 'leading citizens' do. He hires a sad case like Pete. It's not much money, but you know what?"

Gail unpinned the starched white cap and removed it from her head. "What?"

"Pete's got almost enough money saved to get his clarinet out of hock."

Gail felt her eyes growing misty. "Oh, that's wonderful. Did he just tell you that? That's great."

Bruce Cranston grinned. "One of these days, we'll be going out to hear ole Pete at some spiffy club. He's scared, he told me. Afraid he's lost his lip. But he's going to try. That's what counts."

In a sudden burst of enthusiasm, an overflowing of gratitude for the existence of the Bayou Narcotics Rehabilitation Clinic and for the part she was privileged to play in rebuilding the broken lives of unfortunates like Peter Garvey, Gail made a wide, sweeping motion with her arm. "This whole place! It's *all* great! You see such fantastic results from the work you do. You feel — I know this sounds silly to you — I guess you don't get as emotional about it when you've trained at places like the Lexington Center and done clinical research at that big place in Fort Worth and — well, when you're an M.D. But from where *I* sit, it's the most gratifying, fulfilling work."

Bruce laughed. "Second to being instrument nurse for a brain surgeon, right? Isn't that what you used to daydream about?"

"As a probationer, yes," Gail recalled. "In fact, when I was leaving Nebraska and told my folks I was going to work in a New Orleans drug clinic, they acted as though all my training had been a waste of time. I'd built everybody up to imagining me with a surgical mask over my face. My Mom eats up those scenes on TV where the surgeon snaps 'scalpel,' 'suture,' 'clamps.' You know. With the scary tremolo music playing in the background. That's dramatic."

"She was disappointed, huh?" An amused but warm expression made Bruce's face doubly attractive, his deep-blue eyes shining with delight

9

over the imagined scene. "Thought you'd failed her?"

"Terribly," Gail admitted. She could have added that the doctor she had learned to worship wouldn't have fulfilled her mother's requirements for a medical hero, either. Bruce was a bit too thin and rangy. His light-brown hair wasn't neatly groomed, nor was it stylishly long; it was merely a bit on the shaggy side because the young doctor was too busy to have it styled one way or the other. Even now, after having worked under Dr. Cranston's supervision for nearly a year, Gail wasn't sure whether she had fallen in love with him because his handsome appearance had attracted her or that he looked inordinately handsome because she was in love with him.

Appearances, she decided, had little to do with the case; Bruce's good looks were just an extra added bonus. What had won her heart was a cool masculine command of every situation. She had known other doctors with this same assurance about their skill and knowledge, but never before had she encountered in a man this respect-generating quality combined with so much warmth, humility, and compassion. Bruce Cranston was not above saying, "I don't know," and rushing to a medical textbook or a more experienced colleague for information. And there was his kindness with patients — never a lofty, patronizing kindness but a genuine interest, an obvious caring that was reflected in the affection patients had for him. Many a pathetic drug addict, finding himself too weak to continue on the clinic's rehabilitation program, held on, as one had confided in Gail, "because Doc Cranston believes in me. Be a lousy trick to let him down." Bruce could be stern when the occasion demanded a firm hand. But he let it be known that he held a "there, but for the grace of God, go I" attitude toward the men and women who came to the clinic for help.

More than that, Bruce had imbued every nurse, even the part-time scrubwoman, with his philosophy: It was unjust to view the alcoholic as a sick person and to regard the heroin user as a criminal. The Bayou Clinic, partially funded by a philanthropic foundation but depending also on contributions from private parties, had passed the experimental stage. It was doing a job; its operation should be duplicated in every city throughout the land. Unfortunately, it was not. And Bruce thought of his opportunity here as a sacred trust. If the record showed enough success, if the leaders of other communities saw the social and financial advantages, to say nothing of the humanitarian value, of this institution, hundreds of Bayou Clinics *would* spring up in other cities. Instead of wasting millions in courtrooms and jails, the country would be restoring its most pitiful citizens to useful, productive lives. Bruce never stopped pointing out the importance of this collective responsibility. Even the way an orderly said "good morning" to a timorous outpatient could have a bearing on that person's decision to fight or to slide back into the hell of addiction.

But no, Gail decided. These were reasons why she *respected* Bruce. Loving him (and so far she had been obliged to keep her love a secret) was something else again. Perhaps it was a combination of many factors. Or maybe it was simply because Bruce was a man she couldn't *help* falling in love with.

Gail had stepped into the anteroom, which held the nurses' lockers and adjoined the nurses' lounge. It was minutes past five thirty, and she had been on duty since eight, first on the wards among the more difficult new cases that required hospitalization, then, since two o'clock, in one of the two dispensaries. It was here that patients came for their regular dosage of a drug that made it possible for their bodies to function without the ever-increasing need for heroin or morphine, a drug without which they would be plunged back into a choice between the daily struggle to raise enough money for a "fix" or suffering the excruciating agony of withdrawal.

Taking from her locker the pale-green suit she had exchanged this morning for a snugly fitted nylon uniform, Gail called out, "I hope you don't have to work late again, Doctor."

"Not if I can help it," Bruce replied. "I was here until past one this morning. That new case in 209. We had him zapped down with everything in the pharmacopoeia and he still had to be forcibly restrained." With obvious satisfaction, he added, "Doing beautifully today. Gad — twenty-four years old and he's been pushing the stuff for six years. Going to be rough getting that one out of the woods."

Gail lifted a pair of dressy sandals from the locker shelf. She prolonged the moment of parting as long as possible. "Well, get some rest tonight. I'll see you in the morning, Doctor."

"You're in a hurry tonight." Bruce was in the doorway to the locker room. "Heavy date?"

Gail felt herself coloring. "No. No date."

"Whatever happened to — What's-his-name?"

Gail frowned. "Who's that?"

"The fellow who used to work in the lab."

"You don't mean Glenn Reeves?"

"I think that was his name. I know he used to drive you home every evening." Bruce looked uncomfortable, as though he'd gotten into a line of questioning he regretted. "I sort of — assumed he was a — serious . . . Well, you know . . ."

Gail smiled. "He was a serious way of getting home before I could afford a car. Good heavens, Glenn's been in New York for — what is it — four months? Doing graduate work at Columbia."

"Just a casual friend, then?" The doctor's attitude seemed brighter. "I don't know where I got the impression . . ."

The sentence was left hanging, and Gail, feeling a sudden surge of hope, explained, "Glenn's girl-friend helped me find a place to live when I first came to New Orleans. We shared the apartment I'm in now, as a matter of fact. *She* left for New

13

York last month. To be near Glenn."

"Oh. Oh, I see."

Gail couldn't resist laughing at Bruce's expression. He looked like a little boy who had just found the nickel he thought he had lost. "At the moment, I can manage my own transportation. But I can't manage my car payments and keeping up the apartment alone. I s'pose I'll have to look around for someone to share the rent."

"That shouldn't be hard. Mardi Gras time's coming. You can rent out an apple crate during the season. Though — no, you want someone who'd be permanent."

"Actually, I'm enjoying being alone," Gail said. "Indulging myself in a whole month of privacy and quiet." Looking ceilingward for an instant, she recalled, "Glenn's girlfriend had delusions of becoming an opera star. All evening long, la-la-la-la-la. Practicing scales. Joan sounded best in the bathroom. I could never get into the shower 'cause she'd be playing Mimi. Dying of tuberculosis in this *horrible* screeching tone, while I was worried about getting to work late."

It was Bruce's turn to laugh. "That could cure you of a love for opera."

"That whole crazy building could cure me of a lot of things. It's one of those old rambling affairs that's built around a courtyard. And I'll swear the landlord won't rent to anyone unless he, she, or it certifies that he, she, or it is some kind of a nut. Talk about *characters!* It's like a madhouse with magnolias."

14

"And you love it."

Gail nodded. "Adore it. I came from a staid little farming community near North Platte."

"That's in — what? Idaho?"

"Nebraska. My parents run a little variety store there. You can't imagine the contrast."

"I probably can't," Bruce admitted. "My family's been in New Orleans since the Year One. Oh, I've lived in other cities. Med school, interning, residencies in two different states. But my sightseeing was usually confined to the inside of one hospital. This is the only place I know well."

"Is it as romantic to you as it is to a prairie-farmer type like me?"

"Romantic?" Bruce pondered the word for a moment. "If you mean the history, the unique melting-pot aspects of the culture, the quaint old buildings and traditions, yes. I'd use the word 'interesting,' rather than 'romantic.' When you live in a place most of your life and have a houseful of relatives in every other square block, you don't see it the way a tourist does. Of course not. Or when you've worked in a hospital emergency room, especially on Saturday nights, patching up drunks and knifing victims and you-name-it, some of the glamour fades, I guess." Bruce lifted one eyebrow quizzically. "Is that what brought you here?"

Gail suddenly felt like a naïve schoolgirl. "This is going to make a real hayseed out of me, but when I was thirteen, my Aunt Harriet brought me to the Mardi Gras. She'd won two tickets on some

15

sort of quiz show or contest, I forget which. My Uncle Joe couldn't leave his farm at that time of year. Spring. You can imagine. So my aunt decided to take me along. One week, all expenses paid. It couldn't have been much of a prize because we traveled by bus and stayed in this dreary overcrowded hotel. And my aunt was so afraid that the entire male population of the French Quarter was dedicated to snatching her purse and selling her niece into white slavery that we didn't venture out of our hotel room after dark. So I didn't see much. But what I saw left such a lasting impression that — it became an obsession with me."

"To come back here and live?"

"Doesn't that sound crazy?"

"It sounds perfectly logical to me." Bruce grinned. "I had the same kind of mania after seeing a Tarzan movie when I was ten. Except that I never made it to any jungles. You *did* get to New Orleans." He was looking at Gail with a fond approval, the first time, it seemed to her, that the doctor had noticed her as someone other than an efficient co-worker. "You got here, and I'm grateful to Aunt Harriet. Imagine if she had won that prize after the harvest season. Your uncle would have made the trip, and I wouldn't have met you."

Gail dropped her gaze to the floor. She felt awkward, holding her suit and dress shoes in her hands, thrilled by this unexpected personal interest but not knowing what to say.

Bruce saved her by not waiting for a comment. "I don't know how much of the city you've seen. As the old-timers say, if you haven't had dinner at Antoine's or toured Bourbon Street, you haven't been to New Orleans."

"I guess I — haven't been, in that case."

"We could remedy that situation if you aren't busy tonight. You said you didn't have a date."

"I don't."

"Well, I had one, but I've managed to wriggle out of it."

"Oh?"

"Not a date, per se. A committee meeting. My family's been part of the Mardi Gras planning scene for generations back. With my parents hopping around Europe this year, I'd been expected to uphold the family prestige, working on a ball committee. All very intricate and traditional. Lots of protocol, right family, and all that jazz. Frankly, the idea bored me. And then I had an ingenious brainstorm. Why not let my cousin Byron take over for me. You've met Byron."

"I don't think so."

"He's a dentist. He's come to the clinic a few times to look at patients. Anyway, he's big on chairmanships and committees. And status. Fell all over himself when I handed him this headache. So —" Bruce made a relieved shrugging motion. "Instead of sipping tea with dowagers and discussing decorations, I'm free to show you around tonight. We'll cover the places your Aunt Harriet missed."

"It sounds wonderful!" Gail's excitement turned to dismay when she glanced at the simple outfit she had worn to work. "I — wouldn't have time to go home and change, would I? Oh, I'd have to. This old suit . . ."

". . . will probably look great on you."

"No, really. It dates back to my second year in nurse's training. I couldn't go to a fancy place like Antoine's wearing this old rag!"

"All right, I'll pick you up at your apartment. Seven thirty sharp." Bruce shook his head. "Pretty girl like you shouldn't have to worry about . . ."

"Dr. Cranston?"

Gail looked across the dispensary, her glance following Bruce's as Debbie Farraday came hurrying into the room. It would have taken a major catastrophe to ruffle the poise of the day-shift head nurse; with her champagne-colored hair swept back into an elegant chignon, her porcelain-perfect complexion, and her faultless grooming, Miss Farraday was a study in cool perfection. In spite of her calm manner, however, there was no mistaking that she had come to announce an emergency. The quick stride with which she crossed the room was the cue.

"Dr. Cranston, could you come to Admitting right away, please?"

"Got one too hard to handle?" Bruce asked. He had already started for the door.

"The police just brought this patient in," Miss Farraday said in her composed tone. "She's more dead than alive."

18

"Overdose?" Bruce called back.

The head nurse had started to follow him. "Could be that, too. Someone worked her over. She's beaten black and blue."

At the door, Bruce turned to address Gail. "Better come, too, Miss Arnold. What with this being changing-of-the-guard time, we may need all the help we can get."

Gail hastily returned the street clothes to the locker. Minutes later, she joined Dr. Cranston and head nurse Farraday in the Emergency Room next to the Administration office. Two nurses had already placed the patient on a gurney and were pushing the rolling stretcher into the room.

For the next few minutes, first, while Bruce and a resident, Dr. Westbrook, made a hasty examination, then, while emergency orders were barked out, Gail was too busy to closely survey the patient. It was later, when the beating victim had been treated for shock, given a series of injections, and placed in the clinic's intensive-care unit, that Gail was able to observe that the object of this frantic attention was (1) very young, (2) in spite of her bruised and swollen face, probably exceptionally lovely, and (3) as Miss Farraday had said, more dead than alive.

As she adjusted the oxygen mask, Gail brushed back a blood-caked tangle of fiery red hair from the young woman's forehead. There was a scalp laceration that would need attention. Bruce was intent on more immediate concerns. "Get a type and cross-match," he ordered one of the other nurses. The blood sample was drawn, and the doctor specified the number of units he wanted for a blood transfusion. One of the nurses raced out of the room. Miss Farraday brought the I.V. stand closer to the bed.

Working beside the senior doctor, Dr. Westbrook asked, "Why do you suppose the cops brought her here? They were closer to regular hospitals. I mean, from where I understand she was found."

Gail had helped one of the other nurses cut away the girl's blood-stained sweater. They were slipping a hospital gown over her upper body when Bruce said, "They must have gotten a look at her arms, Bill."

Dr. Westbrook leaned forward for a closer look and released a low whistling sound. "My God! Another human pin cushion."

"Both arms," Bruce reminded him.

Gail felt a nauseous churning in her stomach. She should have been inured by this time to the telltale evidence that identified a longtime user. Yet her reaction was always the same: *Why? In the name of heaven, why did you choose to do this to yourself?* No question that this patient had been "shooting junk" with a hypodermic needle for a long period of time. Inflammations had made it difficult for her to find an accessible vein, but the daily search for a place where the syringe could be plunged was a minor agony compared with not having that shot at all.

There was a soft moan from the patient — iron-

20

ically, an encouraging sign. Gail completed her task, handling the girl's arms as gently as possible.

"We're going to want Xrays," Bruce muttered. "Hate to move her, but there may be internal bleeding. Surprised we don't find any fractures. Somebody pounded the daylights out of this poor kid." He made a disgusted sound. "Foot and fist." He glanced up at Miss Farraday. "Any idea who she is?"

"The officers said there wasn't anything to identify her," Miss Farraday said in her toneless voice. "They're waiting outside, Doctor, if . . ."

"No time now," Bruce said. "I just wondered about notifying her next of kin." He was lifting the patient's eyelids, examining her pupils. After a lengthy silence, he said, "The beating was just a *coup de grâce,* I guess. Among the other fights on our hands is counteracting a massive overdose of heroin or morphine. Won't know until we hear from the lab."

Without knowing which of the opium derivatives was involved, Bruce had already started this process in the emergency room. The patient's moan, a minute ago, had been the first indication that stimulants had started to combat her death-like coma.

The evening shift had been on for over an hour before Bruce found the time to remind Gail that she was supposed to have been off duty at five thirty.

"I haven't been in your way, have I?" she asked. It was a facetious question; the doctor had kept four nurses hopping since the unidentified patient was admitted. Now, standing next to the coffee machine near the nurses' station, Gail, the head nurse, and Bruce Cranston were taking their first break.

Bruce indulged himself in a tired smile. "You've been a great help. You know I appreciate your staying."

"And I do, too, of course." Debbie Farraday gave Gail a patronizing nod of approval.

"Gail's had quite a workout," Bruce said. "After being geared for a fabulous dinner at Antoine's. I'm sorry, Gail. We'll make it up another time."

"It couldn't be helped," Gail assured him. Miss Farraday's shoulders had stiffened, and Gail sensed a sudden chill in the atmosphere.

"Those pictures should be developed now," the head nurse said. She drained her styrofoam cup and dropped it into the waste bin. Was it only Gail's imagination, or was it a gesture indicating suppressed anger? "I'll get back to the room if you want to check the Xrays." A condescendingly cool half-smile was turned at Gail. "I expect you'll want to go home, dear. Unless Dr. Cranston thinks otherwise?"

"I think we can manage," Bruce said. "Thank you, Gail. See you in the morning."

He was being considerate, Gail knew. Still, she felt a swift pang of resentment. It was as though fighting for this patient's life was suddenly a private matter that excluded her. It was a shoddy comparison to make, but it was like being asked to leave a dramatic movie just before the climax. As Dr. Westbrook had said, the next few hours would be critical. If the battered young woman survived the night, there would be a better than even chance of saving her. What was done for her this evening would be the key.

Gail left the clinic shortly afterward, stopping at a newstand on her way home to pick up the *Times-Picayune*. During a hastily thrown together dinner alone in her apartment, she scanned the newspaper. But there was no mention of the girl who had been found in a drugged stupor, beaten to a pulp and left to die in a seldom traversed alley. According to the police, it had been amazing that the rooming-house owner who made the shocking discovery had been able to see the victim at all. And it was very unusual, he had told the police, for him to carry out trash at that hour. Had he seen the girl the next morning, which was when he usually deposited garbage in the row of cans behind his building, the victim would have undoubtedly been dead.

No word about the case. Maybe it was too early for a report, Gail decided. Or perhaps the finding of an overdosed junkie was so common that it was no longer regarded as news. Gail set the paper aside, breathed a silent prayer for the girl, and tried to turn her thoughts to more pleasant matters. *Bruce.* Had his mistaken idea that Glenn Reeves was a steady boyfriend been all that kept Bruce from showing a personal interest in her? He had actually asked her for a date. What's more, he had promised to make up for tonight's change in plans.

Gail's excitement was tempered for a moment when she recalled Miss Farraday's reaction. Was the aloof blonde in love with Bruce? More important, had she gotten encouragement from the doctor? No way of knowing. Debbie Farraday was the poor man's Greta Garbo, a sphinx, deliberately mysterious about her personal life.

Once in a while, usually when you wanted to read during lunch, the attractive head nurse would break her customary silence, sit herself down at your table, and subject you to the most unbelievable trivia! Her adventures in trying to exchange a blouse at a department store; the progress of a hurricane off the coast of Mexico; her contempt for price tags that read $49.95, instead of $50, in an attempt to deceive you into thinking you were "spending in the forties instead of the fifties." These were the inane topics on which Debbie Farraday expounded. Her personal life, her philosophies, her views on important issues (if, indeed, she gave them any thought at all) were question marks. None of the nurses who worked under Miss Farraday's efficient supervision had the faintest idea of where she lived, what constituted her social life, what she thought. Hence, it was entirely possible that her relationship with Bruce Cranston was, or had been, more than casual. If so, it might be unpleasant to work for her after tonight.

Gail shrugged off the faintly irritating thought.

Down in the courtyard, the three latest zany additions to the old apartment building were making an ear-splitting ruckus with tambourines, a flute, and a homemade instrument that looked as if it had been constructed after a visit to a plumber's scrap heap. Maybe they were rehearsing a Mardi Gras stunt. Whatever their plans, the din was unbearable.

Gail closed the French windows leading to her tiny balcony and flicked on the television, the sole furnishing in the room that she could call her own (graduation gift from Uncle Joe and Aunt Harriet). Apparently the network newscast had been concluded; an announcer was giving a capsule view of the local news.

Before she flicked off the set, Gail knew only that the new patient at the Bayou Clinic was still alive, though her condition was listed as critical; that the young woman had taken or been given a lethal dose of heroin; and that a police officer had identified her as a former "exotic dancer" and habitué of New Orleans' seamier night spots. Her name was Stella De Shiel.

If she had any relatives or friends, none had come to claim her, nor were there any missing persons reports matching Stella De Shiel's description.

Two

A full week had gone by during which time Bruce Cranston had devoted the majority of his time to Stella De Shiel. "And I can do without a repeat of anything like the last seven days," he told Gail one morning.

"You've brought her through," Gail reminded him. "That should compensate for some of your exhaustion."

He was bone weary, but Bruce managed an appreciative smile. "Thanks. It does. And what a fantastic education I've gotten! Here you are with a patient that's too debilitated to be able to withstand even the mildest withdrawal symptoms. You've got to keep her going, but the problems of keeping her in physiological balance . . . whew! I questioned every move I made. Double-thought every decision. And just between us I made a few lucky guesses."

"Modesty, modesty." Gail laughed softly. "Frankly, I think you performed a minor miracle. None of us gave that girl a prayer when we first saw her."

Bruce glanced toward the maximum-care ward. "Stella's far from being in the pink of condition. I don't mean the bruises. She's on the mend physically. A good, wholesome diet will get some weight on her, fill out the hollows, and get her over that deathly pallor. Typical junkie — she was so undernourished it was pitiful. But that's not what I mean."

"I've been with her every day," Gail pointed out. "You don't have to explain."

"You have to have cooperation to pull them out of addiction," Bruce said. He apologized quickly. "You know that. I'm not giving you a beginner's course in the subject. It's more like talking to myself."

Gail understood. "I can understand your frustration. All the dilaudid in the world isn't going to help Stella kick the habit if she doesn't make up her mind that she wants to. But doesn't it make sense that she *would* want to? After the close call she's just had? Just the fear of having it happen again."

"Whatever did happen," Bruce said absently.

"They still don't know, do they? The police?"

"They haven't gotten any clues from Stella, that's for sure. She clams up . . . well, you know. She hasn't talked to you either, has she?"

Gail shook her head. "Just lies there like a vegetable, staring at the ceiling."

"Except when someone walks into the room," Bruce said. "And then she jumps. She's not lethargic, Gail. She's very *much* aware of what's going on around here. Jumpy. That's par for the course. But I sense a hostility."

"You haven't had any touching words of gratitude for saving her life?" Gail knew better; it was a sarcastic question.

"I haven't had an answer when I've said 'good morning'."

"It could be fear," Gail suggested.

"Fear of the police, maybe. But of *us?*"

Gail shrugged. "Soon as she's stronger, you can let Dr. Praeger figure it out. I know I'm tired of playing staff psychiatrist. Stella's probably sick in a way that I can't help. Although . . ." Gail hesitated.

"Although what?"

"I've tried going on the theory that Stella's paralyzed with fear of everybody. After all, she's gone through a horrible experience. The trauma after someone's tried to murder you . . ."

"Could have been just a domestic battle," Bruce argued. "Boyfriend got jealous and decided to beat her up. Maybe the overdose of heroin was a suicide attempt. The police have considered that, you know. They even wondered if she could have sustained her injuries in a fall. Doped up, staggering through the alley . . ."

"*Could* it have been that? A series of falls — hitting her face on those garbage cans or against the cement?"

"Possible," Bruce said, "but not probable. My point is, I'm dubious about the murder-attempt theory. Seems to me if Stella were afraid of someone, she'd be babbling every detail of what happened to her to the cops. And begging us to cure her. Straighten out her life."

Gail agreed, then added, "Speaking of straight-ening out her life, she's due for medication right now."

"Medication she gets, conversation you don't get. Right?"

Miss Farraday appeared in the hall with a problem that demanded Dr. Cranston's imme-diate attention. Was it coincidence or did these "you must come with me at once, Doctor" prob-lems arise only when Gail was enjoying a few pre-cious moments alone with him?

Bruce had been too busy to suggest that he and Gail make up for their interrupted date, but ap-parently Debbie Farraday hadn't forgotten about it. Yesterday, during lunch, the head nurse had joined Gail at her table and made at least three comparisons between the clinic cafeteria and the city's most celebrated eating establishment. Subtle attempts at prying, at first. Trying to open a discussion by saying things like, "At Antoine's, they wouldn't serve a salad this wilted to the gar-bage disposal," and, "At Antoine's, it deserves to be called vichyssoise. Here, it's just plain old po-tato soup, isn't it?" When these ploys had failed to get the desired result, Miss Farraday, pretending only a casual interest, asked the direct question: "You *have* had dinner there, haven't you? At Antoine's?"

Miss Farraday didn't sigh with relief when Gail had replied in the negative, but she dropped the subject immediately afterward. Gail had felt an urge to say, "No, I haven't gone out on a date with

Bruce Cranston. But when I do, I'll be sure to tell you all the details. Better still, I'll invite you to come along as a chaperone." She had resisted the impulse, of course. And, later she had regretted even her inner resentfulness. Maybe Debbie Farraday was finally coming out of her aloof shell, exhibiting a normal curiosity about the people she worked with. I could just be projecting this jealousy on her part, Gail had decided.

Now she was less sure of that decision as the head nurse led Dr. Cranston off toward her office. Gail sighed and made her way to the medicine cabinet, unlocking the door, taking out the sedative prescribed for Stella De Shiel, and then heading for the latter's room.

There was no change in Stella's customary reaction when Gail stepped into the pleasantly furnished quarters. The red-haired patient jerked to a sitting position on her bed, a painful move, considering her bruised body.

"It's only me," Gail chirped. "Time for your happy pill." She smiled broadly, her lighthearted attitude as deliberate as the room's sunny decor. Every effort had been made to furnish the patient's quarters with homey touches and cheerful colors, erasing the cold (and, to an addict, frightening), antiseptic effect of a hospital.

Stella released her suspended breath and slowly sank her head back to the pillow. But her dark-lashed green eyes were still wide with alarm, and her heart was palpitating so fiercely that its motion quivered her hospital gown. As Gail poured a glass of water and then handed her a tiny paper cup containing her medication, Stella eyed the pill with distrust.

"It's all right," Gail assured her. "My goodness, honey, how are we going to convince you that we're all your friends here? Every time the door opens, you jump. When actually every person who enters your room is coming in with something that's going to help you get well. A good meal, something to calm your nerves, a bath tray. All positive things, Stella. Go on. Gulp her down."

Stella obeyed, raising herself up and placing the pill in her mouth, then accepting the water glass slowly. When the pill had been swallowed, she leaned back again, closing her eyes. Gail noticed that her hands trembled convulsively during the process.

"Atta girl. That should make you feel better." Gail didn't expect a response, nor did she get one. Standing beside the bed, she surveyed Stella's face.

There were still abundant signs of a savage beating; purplish blue circles around her eyes and a swollen lower lip were the most obvious mementos. In spite of this, it was apparent that Stella was an uncommonly beautiful young woman. She had the finely molded features of a fashion model — a slender, delicately sculpted nose, perfectly delineated lips. With her eyelids lowered, the bruises dominated her face. But Gail imagined how she would look in a week or so, the dark swellings gone and the long dark lashes fluttering over those arresting eyes, uniquely colored to re-semble pale-green gemstones.

Stella's hair had been shampooed, more for sanitary than for cosmetic or morale-building reasons. With the blood and grime removed, the copper-colored mane cascaded down to within a half an inch of her shoulders. When Gail had first seen it, she would have sworn that this distinctive metallic shade was created in a chemical lab. Not so. Stella's hair, fiery with golden highlights in spite of her generally poor state of health, was the real McCoy. Lovely. Probably too beautiful for her own good. If Stella had been just another brown-eyed brunette with unspectacular features like me, Gail thought, she might have joined a sec-retarial pool, married some nice, dependable me-chanic, and raised a couple of equally unspectacular kids in a suburban-tract home. Being beautiful (and knowing this was inescap-able), Stella had chosen what was to her a predes-tined, glamorous course. With talent, luck, or a little of each, she might have become a film star. She had instead found herself dancing in a cheap club, a meeting place for unsavory characters. The drug route had not been inevitable. Nor had it been a difficult path to find in that atmosphere.

Stella wasn't asleep; she was just pretending to be. "Well, I can see that you'd rather be alone," Gail said. "So I'll be getting on my horse. OK?"

Surprisingly, the girl's eyes opened wide. "Don't go!" Stella whispered. "Please don't leave me alone."

"I can stay for a *bit*," Gail told her. She was enormously pleased to have gotten any kind of response from this strangely uncommunicative patient. "I have other patients to look after, though. And since you don't seem to want company . . ."

"Oh, I do." Stella's voice had a deep, raspy quality like the hoarse, breathless tone of a movie sex symbol. "I want you to stay. I'm — I'm scared to be here by myself." She pulled herself upright. "Look. Look, I'll sit up and talk to you. Is that what you want? I'll tell you anything you want to know."

Gail patted the girl's wrist. "I don't want to grill you, Stella. I'd just like to be your friend. I mean, since we're stuck with seeing each other every day, doesn't it make sense for us to be friends?"

Stella looked bewildered for a moment, as though friendship were an alien concept. Then she said, "Is the door locked?"

"Locked? No, why should it be? We trust you, Stella. You've gotten through the worst part of withdrawal. Thanks to your doctor, it wasn't the ordeal it might have been."

Stella nodded, perhaps not quite comprehending that new drugs and new techniques had taken her through the hell every junkie dreaded, the first days without a fix.

"So you aren't going to run away somewhere, are you? Not when Dr. Cranston's gotten you this far along. Not when you know there's a wonderful life ahead for you if you stay and — what's the term? — if you get the monkey off your back."

33

A mist formed over those strangely beautiful eyes. "It doesn't matter anymore."

"Whether you get free of heroin? You know it matters, Stella! And that's why we don't have to lock the door to keep you here. You've come to a rare spot, old girl. One of the most progressive, best-equipped . . ."

"They aren't going to leave me alone." Stella spoke in a brooding monotone. "They'll get me. What difference will it make if I'm on the stuff or off? I'll be just as dead, either way." She looked up, her eyes meeting Gail's, reflecting a terror that must have been excruciating. "I'm not worried about me going out that door. I'm scared of someone else coming in."

"Who?"

Stella shook her head, her swollen lips clamped together tightly.

"Who would want to hurt you, Stella? Who *did* try to kill you? If the police knew that, they'd get whoever did it. He'd be in jail, and you wouldn't have to . . ."

"He'd be in jail. Sure. His word against mine. Do you think any judge is going to take a junkie's word against that of a . . ." Stella broke off her sentence. "Look — what's your name? I don't even know what to call you."

"Gail. Gail Arnold."

"Gee, that's pretty. Gail Arnold."

For a second, Gail thought the lovely redhead was going to cry. Stella composed herself. "I shouldn't be telling you all this."

"Yes, you should. It's bothering you, Stella. Whatever it is, get it off your mind."

The pill was beginning to take effect, and Stella yawned. Her voice drowsy, she said, "This is — I don't want the fuzz to know this. If they thought I squealed to the fuzz, they'd get me for sure. They'll probably get me, anyway. But — maybe if I get — cured — I could go someplace. Some other country, maybe. You could put the word out that I died. If they thought I was dead, I'd be all right, wouldn't I? Just — if I can just stay alive long enough to get off the junk. Really off."

It was the first time anyone had heard Stella express a determination to free herself of her addiction. Gail could hardly wait to report the news to Bruce Cranston. She would have a report to make to Dr. Praeger, too. Leave it to the staff psychiatrist to determine whether Stella De Shiel's fears were grounded in fact or whether she was suffering from a deeply rooted paranoia. The important thing now was that she was communicating. Gail encouraged the unexpected breakthrough. "You keep referring to 'them,' Stella. You keep saying 'they.' Who are you talking about?"

Stella's eyes were closed again, her head nestled against the propped-up pillow. Like a psychiatric patient arrested in a trancelike state of recalling the past, she droned, "I fell in love with this man. I was working at . . . I thought it was a fabulous place at the time. Now I know it was just a crummy dive. The Cinderbox. But I thought I was in heaven. Four hundred bucks for a costume that wasn't anything but a few yards of fringe and some sequins. Guys applauding, wanting to buy me drinks, I thought I was really somebody. Thought I knew all the answers, too. And then along comes this man. Real class. Y'know? I fell on my face, I was so crazy about him."

Gail could have taken the story from there, for it was a typical case history. Stella's lover had started her on "joy-popping." A shot of heroin used only once in a while, strictly for "kicks," was all right, wasn't it? It hadn't been all right. It had been all wrong, as Stella discovered when she learned that she was hooked, that her body chemistry had been altered so that heroin was as necessary to her as breathing air.

"I was at a point where I had to come up with seventy-five dollars every day," Stella went on. "That's seventy-five in cash each and every day. I wasn't earning that kind of money at the club. Anyway, I got fired. My boss didn't mind taking a cut for the pushers who used his place as a contact, but he wasn't having any part of showgirls with needlemarks on their arms."

"What did you do?" Gail asked.

There were only three alternatives; crime, prostitution, or getting others hooked on narcotics. Stella had been induced by her "friend" to start pushing dope. "I was a big success," Stella said bitterly. "Not only being sure of my own supply but making money. Clothes! You should have seen me go wild in the swanky shops around town. Gifts for my friends. Wow, I laid out six hundred clams for a watch on Tim's birthday."

"Tim. That was . . ."

Stella hesitated. "Yeah, that was his name. Past tense. He died of an overdose just about a week after he turned thirty. Funny. I didn't go to pieces. A fix fixes everything, like he used to say. He was the most important person in my life, and I didn't even cry at the funeral. All alone in the world, and I didn't care."

"Don't you have a family? Parents — brothers or sisters?"

Stella was silent for a moment before replying, "No." She turned over on her side, changing the subject with equal abruptness. Or, more accurately, she returned to her subject. After days of sullen silence, it was as though a dam had burst inside Stella De Shiel and her life depended on this outpouring of words. Perhaps, Gail decided, it *did*.

"I was pushing for what I thought was a big operation. Just like in the gangster movies. You know. I only had one contact, and he probably only knew one other guy in the organization. You're not supposed to know who the big boss is." Stella swallowed hard. "I found a notebook in one of Tim's suits after he died. A whole list of dealers and their phone numbers. One guy I had met, Louie LaFollette, recited seven or eight of the names from memory. I didn't find out the name of the top guy until just before those three hoods broke into my pad and started to beat me up. They could have killed me with one punch, but I figure that wasn't the idea. They wanted it to look like maybe I took an accidental overdose and fell down."

"They must have been pretty sure you were going to die," Gail said.

"Yeah, they were. Otherwise, they wouldn't have told me Virgil Corbett sent them."

"Who's he?"

"Guy who owns a string of clubs. Fronts."

"But if you were doing such a good job for him, why would he want you killed?"

"I had a better offer," Stella said. From her tone she could have been a salesgirl considering a move to a department store that offered more fringe benefits. "The syndicate's moving in big. When they contacted me, I figured I didn't have much choice. Might as well work for the biggest. Y'know? Especially when you know they're going to wipe out the small fry sooner or later. So I said, sure, why not? Count me in. I should have demanded protection."

Stella's tale was beginning to resemble a gangster movie made in the forties, one that Gail had seen once on the Late Late Show. Convincing as she sounded, there was a melodramatic quality about her story. She was sick; drugs had taken their toll inside her muddled brain. Was she just dramatizing herself, playing the leading role in a plot filled with intrigue?

Gail decided that she was, a few minutes later, when Stella whispered, "The guy who approached me said I wouldn't have to worry about getting busted, pushing for his outfit. The big wheel has too much power. Respectable businessman. Political connections. Money for payoffs. They're *so* big they don't even have to be careful. Like I *know* who runs the drug traffic for the big mob."

Gail was convinced by now that her patient was suffering from delusions. She didn't encourage the fantasy by asking for the name.

Stella supplied it anyway. "Paul Mascon. That's who it is. R. Paul Mascon."

Under other circumstances Gail would have laughed out loud. It was obvious where Stella had gotten the name for the chief villain in her story. It was printed in raised letters on a small plaque at the side of the door. Owner of a large real estate, mortgage, and insurance company, Mascon was the philanthropist who had donated funds for this entire wing of the clinic! Stella had probably seen his name dozens of times, for the bronze inscriptions were to be found throughout this ward.

Nothing could be served by arguing with a patient who lived in a dream world of her own fabrication. Gail made a mental note to tell Dr. Praeger about this conversation, then asked a logical question: "If you're afraid of these people, why don't you tell all this to the police?"

Stella's hands gripped the edge of her sheet. "They wouldn't believe Mascon's a drug czar. Anyway, I don't want anybody to know how much *I* know."

"You just told me," Gail reminded her.

For a few seconds she thought Stella was going to break down in sobs. The agony on that bruised but still beautiful face was indescribable. Then, her voice a pathetic whimper, she said, "I shouldn't have told you. I — you said you were my friend. I needed to tell *somebody.* Listen. Listen, forget it. Forget the names. *Especially the names.* They'll be out to get me, but if they know I told you about Virgil Corbett, they'd shut you up, too. They're vicious. You don't know. You don't know how vicious."

Stella started to weep softly after that, blurting out a repeated request that Gail forget everything she had heard. Knowing that a paranoid's delusions are every bit as terrifying as fears based on reality, Gail assured the girl that the conversation would be forgotten. Because Stella begged her to stay, Gail did so, waiting for the tranquilizer to take effect.

Later, the staff psychiatrist could tackle this complex imaginary plot of battling gangs and narcotics rings headed by prominent citizens. A nurse was not qualified to judge or to attempt tearing down something that might be partially true and had been distorted by a seriously disturbed mind. There was no way to allay Stella De Shiel's fears except to remain at her side.

Even this was not enough. When she was finally convinced that Stella was asleep, Gail started out of the room. She was startled by a distraught plea from her patient: "Couldn't you lock the door? Let me lock the door from the inside? Please.

Please tell Dr. Cranston they're going to come and kill me!"

"I'll talk to the doctor," Gail promised. She hoped that Stella's paranoiac fear would disappear as her general health improved and reminded herself to explain the girl's apprehension to Bruce.

That Stella had no reason for fear was evidenced by the fact that no one seemed interested in her presence at the clinic. There had been no telephone calls to ask about her, no get-well cards in the mail, no visitors. Now that she was recovering, the news media, perhaps even the police, had lost interest in her. It was understandable, perhaps, that someone as completely alone in the world as Stella would invent an exciting drama that revolved around her. There was no question that she was mixed up with unwholesome characters, that she had probably taken a shoddy eruption of violence and, consciously or otherwise, magnified it to heroic proportions. One thing seemed fairly certain: From the absence of interest in Stella De Shiel, there were no enemies against whom her door had to be locked. Unfortunately, neither were there any friends.

Three

Gail had been wrong. Stella De Shiel *did* have someone who cared about her. But when Charlie De Shiel came to see her several days later, the patient refused to see him.

"I'm sorry," Gail was forced to tell Stella's father. "She said she doesn't want anyone to come into her room. We don't want to upset her. And she was . . ." Gail glanced at Bruce Cranston, who had gone to the room with her in an attempt at persuading Stella to admit her visitor. "She was getting hysterical."

"It might be best to wait until she's feeling better," Bruce said kindly. "Stella's very confused. Don't take it personally."

They were standing in the reception room, Mr. De Shiel nervously turning the rim of a blue captain's hat in his work-worn hands. A stocky, muscular figure probably in his late fifties, the man who had introduced himself as Stella's father was shy and soft-spoken. He had the weather-beaten face of a man who has long worked out of doors, and he appeared to be uncomfortable in the outdated blue suit he had put on for the occasion. Neither his close-cropped iron-gray hair nor his wide sun-bronzed features would have associated him with his daughter. But there was no question from which parent Stella had inherited her unique green eyes.

Those eyes looked clouded now with a touching sorrow. "You told her it was her daddy?" he asked. Then, immediately, he said, "Sure you did. Didn't mean to doubt you, miss. Or you, Doctor."

"Dr. Cranston's right, Mr. De Shiel. You mustn't feel hurt. Your daughter's just gone through a terrible experience and she's — well, it's not because she doesn't want to see you. She's frightened and bewildered. Maybe ashamed, too. Try to understand."

"It's the drugs," Mr. De Shiel muttered. "I understand, all right, miss. Stella wouldn't see me when I came lookin' for her that first time she ran away from home. Lord, she wasn't sixteen yet."

A loudspeaker called for Dr. Cranston, and Stella's father said, "I won't hold you folks no longer. I know you got work to do. And I sure do thank you for all your trouble. All you're doing for my little girl."

"I do have to get to the dispensary," Bruce said. "Miss Arnold's on her break, though. Why don't you have coffee together?" Gail's puzzlement, since she was definitely on duty, was cleared up in Bruce's next sentence. "We've known absolutely nothing about Stella's background. It would help us if we knew more about her, Mr. De Shiel. Maybe you could tell Miss Arnold something that would be of value."

"Well, sure," Mr. De Shiel said. "Any way I can help. I don't know much about psychology and what have you, not havin' no education you can speak of, but I know you people like to find out maybe why a person got to takin' drugs. Like maybe the way I raised Stella. It could be that."

Bruce caught the miserable catch in the other man's voice and gave him a reassuring pat on the shoulder. "I doubt it," he said. "Talk to Miss Arnold anyway. She can tell you about Stella's progress, too."

Bruce's reasoning was sound, but Gail suspected that he was also concerned about sending Charlie De Shiel away from the clinic emotionally empty-handed. He had come to New Orleans from Biloxi, out of which he operated a "fleet" of two shrimp boats. His anxiety when he had finally heard the news about Stella, his preparations, his suspense before he reached this place, would be for nothing if he were to leave now. He hadn't seen his daughter, and a conversation with someone who was in daily contact with her would be a small consolation prize. But it would be better than nothing. It was typical of Bruce to sense this and to react with compassion.

Minutes later, over coffees at the small counter just off the clinic's main reception room, Gail realized how badly Stella's father needed someone to talk to. Guilt-ridden, his eyes rarely met hers. She had never felt as sorry for narcotics addicts as she felt for those who loved them and watched helplessly while they destroyed themselves. Mr.

De Shiel's misery was compounded by a conviction that he was somehow to blame, which made him even more pitiable.

"When Stella's mama died, she — our little girl — wasn't no more'n nine years old. Well, I tried to be Stella's ma *and* pa, but y'know it's hard for a man. I was pretty broke up after I lost Margie. Maybe I didn't do right. Thinkin' about how bad I felt, maybe not sayin' the right things to Stella. I just kinda — well, I'm not much for pretty words — I just kinda put my arms around Stella and tried to make it better."

"I'm sure you did everything you could," Gail said.

The man shook his head. "I don't know. It wasn't too bad 'til Stella started growin' up. I was gone a lot. Out on the boat. Couldn't help that. It's how I make a livin', and I don't know no other way. Trouble is, Stella was all by herself too much. Started runnin' around. And pretty. I tell you, there was times I wished she'd looked like me 'stead of her mama. All the boys chasin' her, and folks tellin' her she ought to be a movie star, she ought to be somewhere in a big city where she'd make it big. That's all Stella talked about. After a while, seems like the two of us was just — like strangers."

"Mr. De Shiel, all parents have that problem." Gail smiled her reassurance. "At sixteen, I thought my folks weren't quite bright, that they couldn't possibly understand me. It's a natural part of growing up."

45

"It don't help none to know that," Mr. De Shiel said. "Sure, I *knew* what kids are like. But that time Stella run off here to New Orleans, I came up trampin' the streets lookin' for her, clean out of my mind I was so scared. Well, that time the police found her an' I got her back home. But I knew I wasn't goin' to keep her home. I just kept waitin' for the day she'd run off again."

"And she did."

"Well, yes, miss, she did. And it wasn't 'til the last time when I couldn't get her back. She was legal age then. Still a little kid, far as knowin' what was good for her, but nothin' I could do but come beggin' for her to leave that fella. That no-good devil what got her started takin' drugs. Not to speak bad of the dead, but he was 'bout as rotten a man ever walked God's green earth."

"It sounds to me as though you did everything you could," Gail offered.

Mr. De Shiel sighed. "I don't know. I think back an' I wonder — if I hadn't been so stubborn, sayin' there'd never be another woman like Stella's mama, nobody as could ever take her place — I might have found me a nice wife. My little girl would have come home from school and had somebody there. House all neat an' clean. Lady to make dresses an' do all the things a girl likes. Things a man couldn't do even if he wanted to."

Gail stirred her coffee absently. "I think you're blaming yourself for something that wasn't your fault," she said. "We get patients here who've had every advantage, all the things you seem to think Stella missed."

The man was only faintly encouraged. "You can't keep lookin' back and askin' yourself where you failed," he said. "Thing I wanted to say, though, you guessed right about Stella not wantin' to see me 'cause she's ashamed. It was the same way every time I'd come to the city an' look her up. After, I'd give up tryin' to talk her into comin' home. What kind of home did I have for a pretty young girl makin' good money dancin' in some fancy place? I knew better'n that. By that time I was only tryin' to stop her from wreckin' her health with that poison. Get her away from — all those bad people. Never would see me. About broke my heart."

"There's one ray of hope," Gail said. "She knows now that you were giving her good advice. Stella's moved a lot closer to you, Mr. De Shiel."

The green eyes met Gail's, reflecting gratitude. "I sure enough do hope you're right, miss."

"I know I'm right. If Stella didn't realize how wrong she's been, she wouldn't be ashamed to face you, would she?"

"You think there's a chance she'll — get cured?"

"Nobody can promise that," Gail said. "But she's getting the finest care possible. It takes a long time to erase the damage of a long-lasting heroin habit. Actually, patients aren't ever cured. But their dependency can be arrested. If they're determined to free themselves of addiction, we have drugs now that can help them. Their own determination. That's the key. Without that, there's nothing a doctor can do."

"You think maybe Stella . . ."

"She's still too sick and bewildered to make any strong stand," Gail said. "Right now, while she's here, you don't have to worry about her. She's making progress, as the doctor told you."

Charlie De Shiel rapped his knuckles against the Formica counter. "If she could just get over the habit. Get away from that crowd of riffraff. I tell you, if I could see Stella married to some nice young man, leadin' a happy life, I wouldn't care if she *never* let me see her again." He was shaking his head, staring into his barely touched cup of coffee, when he added, "I made plenty of mistakes, but one thing I can say. Stella learned about what's right and what's wrong. I never smoked or drank or gambled. Didn't chase women. Never. Grew up on the wharfs. Worked hard all my life and seen bad times. Seen it all, you might say." He looked up, his expression begging Gail to believe him. "I tried to be a good father, though. If I made mistakes, it was 'cause I'm just a ignorant workin' man. I meant to do right."

Gail did her best to assure him that no one blamed him for the course his daughter had chosen and that he shouldn't blame himself. After that, he asked questions about Stella: How did she look, what did she talk about, in what *ways* was she making progress?

Gail filled him in on every detail, dredging her

48

mind for positive reports but being careful not to build false hopes of a miraculous "cure" or to step into the medical provinces that were beyond her scope as a nurse.

It had been a good idea to talk to the man, she decided. Stella's father seemed, if not more cheerful, at least not as depressed as when he had first appeared at the nurses' station and identified himself. Stella's refusal to see him, though it was not a new experience, had been a crushing blow. But the shrimp-boat captain appeared more at ease now, convinced that his "little girl" was in good hands. He had only one request to make, and he made that humbly: "I know you got lots to do, miss. Important things to do. If you could just talk to Stella, though. Tell her I don't mean to find fault or try to get her to come home. Nothin' like that. Just make her see that I . . ." He seemed to be embarrassed by the tender phrase on his lips.

"That you love her very much," Gail said for him.

Mr. De Shiel nodded. "That's it. Tell her that, will you please? That all I want is to see her. Friendly visit. Tell her I'll keep callin' to see how she's gettin' along, but I won't come back 'til she asks me to. Would you do that for me, miss?"

"I would have done it even if you hadn't asked me to," Gail said. "I can't promise results. But I'll keep trying."

"I sure do thank you," Charlie De Shiel said. His coffee had gotten cold, and he pushed it forward on the counter with one hand, the other

49

clutching his cap. As he slipped off the bar stool, he said, "Tell Dr. Cranston I thank him, too. Never *will* be able to tell you folks how much I 'preciate what you're doin' for my girl."

He left the building a few minutes later, a pathetic figure with a shuffling step that, Gail guessed, had once been energetic and proud. At least he wasn't completely hopeless, and he had made a vicarious contact with Stella through her nurse.

Gail's tender feeling toward Mr. De Shiel was overshadowed by her renewed admiration for Bruce Cranston. How deeply he cared for the people who needed him! Not only the victims of drug addiction but those who suffered with them out of love. Gail wondered if she had ever told the doctor how she felt about this trait in him. Why did people withhold compliments, afraid of sounding overly sentimental, so afraid of being called maudlin that praise was saved for eulogies? She decided, at the next opportunity, to tell Bruce, without actually telling him that she loved him, one of the reasons why.

Four

"Nothing every ordinary garden-variety medic wouldn't have done," Bruce said. He was being facetiously modest, pretending he didn't take Gail's compliment seriously. But he was obviously pleased.

Gail had started telling the doctor about her conversation with Stella's father during their late-afternoon session in the dispensary. Caring for outpatients had interrupted her recital so many times that afterward Bruce had suggested that she finish telling him the story during dinner. Not the promised fabulous dinner at Antoine's; he had work to do at the clinic that evening. But if Gail would settle for a little Basque restaurant just around the corner . . .

Gail had been delighted. During dinner, she had filled him in on Stella De Shiel's background. It wasn't until now, as Bruce drove her back to the clinic where her own car was parked, that Gail summoned the courage to tell the doctor how much she admired him for his thoughtfulness.

"You can make funny remarks all you like," she said. "I'm still glad you made up that story about me being on my coffee break. That poor man needed somebody to talk to. Can you imagine the hell he's gone through? His only child sending him away. He had a hard time articulating the way he feels. 'Love' seems a hard word for some people to say."

Bruce turned his eyes from the street for a brief moment. "It is, isn't it? I wonder why?"

"I guess we're all cautious about surrendering ourselves, making that total commitment, 'cause we're afraid of not being loved back. Rough on the ego."

"You're probably right. It's a self-protective instinct."

"I think it comes right after the one we're born with. Fear of falling."

"Same thing," Bruce quipped. "Go on with what you were saying, lady. I could listen to you all night."

Gail laughed. "OK, make fun when somebody tries to tell you you're a wonderful, sensitive person. Next time I'll keep my nice thoughts about you to myself."

Bruce turned the small sedan into the personnel parking area behind the clinic. As he parked his car next to Gail's, he said, "Are you in the habit of having quote-nice-unquote thoughts about me?" He switched off the ignition, turning to fix Gail with a probing stare. "Tell me more."

Gail felt the blood rushing to her face, grateful for the dim light. "I've always thought you were — head and shoulders over most doctors I've known."

"That's good for a start. What else?"

"Well, you're — kind. To everybody. Patients, their relatives."

"Nurses?" Bruce's arm slipped across the back of the car seat. "Ever observed that I'm exceptionally kind to nurses?"

Gail's breath seemed to be caught inside her lungs. "All nurses?"

"Just some. One in particular. And the word isn't 'kindness.' It's something else, Gail. A word — I'm not sure yet, but maybe it's — one of those words we're afraid to say until we're sure of ourselves. Sure of our own feelings, not to mention someone else's."

She was in Bruce's arms, his kiss warm and honest against her lips. Gail found herself clinging to him in a long embrace. It was an endless period in time, and yet it seemed to end too soon, almost as though it had never happened.

If Bruce was as exhilarated by their kiss as Gail was, he managed to pull himself together faster. "That's for having nice thoughts about me. Don't stop. It was beautiful."

There was no commitment there, Gail thought. She felt a vague stirring of disappointment, as though she had only been rewarded for paying an ego-building compliment. Still, Bruce had hinted that it might mean more, hadn't he? He wanted to be sure of himself, sure of her. Should she tell him how *long* she had been in love with him?

She didn't get the chance. Seconds later, an orderly came racing across the parking lot, making his way directly to Bruce's sedan.

"Dr. Cranston." The young man was breathless. "Miss Anderson said she just saw your car pull in. We're having trouble with Miss De Shiel. Dr. Wibberly's busy with an emergency patient — guy freaked out on LSD. Could you . . ."

"Right away." Bruce was already getting out of his car. "What's happening?"

"D.t.'s. She's seeing things, I guess." The orderly turned, hurrying back ahead of the doctor. "We're having a bad time trying to restrain her."

Gail had gotten out of the other side of the car, circling the front to join Bruce. "That's Stella. Should I come, too?"

"You're about the only person who can communicate with her. Yes. Come on."

They rushed across the nearly empty lot to one of the clinic's rear doors, breaking into a run as they followed the corridor to the intensive care unit and heard the tumult. Stella's screams echoed through the wards, shrill with terror.

She was out of her bed, struggling to fight off the orderly and two nurses who were attempting to stop her from racing out of the room. "Let me go!" Stella was crying. "They're coming! They're going to kill me!"

She was beyond kindly reassurances from strangers. Even Bruce Cranston's calm assurance, "No one's going to hurt you, Stella. We're all your friends," had no effect. Wild-eyed, her red hair disheveled, Stella was in the grip of a paranoiac fear that could not be talked away.

54

Gail made an attempt to soothe the terrified patient, but she knew that Stella had passed the stage where words would be effective. Real or imagined, this kind of fright was excruciating. The only solution was chemical.

Bruce had already directed one of the nurses to bring a hypo filled with a drug that would render Stella insensible.

Waiting for the nurse to return made eternity seem understandable, though she was back in the room in a matter of minutes. It meant feeling utterly helpless while you watched a soul in torment. And trying to hold Stella's arms as she flailed them around trying to escape her captors, screaming that she had to get away. They were in league with the people who tried to murder her, Stella sobbed. Her strength, motivated by unreasoning fear, was phenomenal, considering her poor physical condition.

"It's all right, Stella," Gail kept repeating. "Easy now, you're all right. You're safe with us."

"You can't — keep me here!" Stella hurled herself around and tried to reach the door. It took all of Bruce's strength and that of the orderly to stop her. The remaining nurse had been flung against the wall by a vicious swing of Stella's lowered head. Gail gasped in pain as the patient's left hand got free for an instant, long enough to claw her fingernails across Gail's neck.

Subduing Stella long enough for Bruce to plunge the needle into her arm was a nightmare. She fought, accused Gail and the doctor of lying to her, pleaded wildly for them not to kill her. In her experience at the clinic, Gail had never witnessed a more pitiful sight.

"We're going to move you out of this room," Bruce said when the calming drug had been injected. "A *safer* room. No one can get to you. We're your friends. We'll protect you, dear."

Bruce's words were drowned out by Stella's hysterical cries. In her delusion, she was being murdered; her fate had been sealed by the needle she had fought against like a wild animal. Now she dissolved in wracking sobs. "Why did you — do it? I don't — want to die. Oh, God, please — please, please, please, I don't — I can't — ohh, no, no, *please!*"

"You aren't going to die," Bruce told her. He was experienced enough to know that his pacifying speech was futile, but no one with a heart could have acted otherwise. "We love you, Stella. All of us here love you and want you to get well. We won't let anybody harm you. When you wake up, you'll be in another room. Your enemies won't know where to find you. Ever."

Was he telling Stella that he had decided that the clinic was unable to cope with her case? That she would have to be committed to a psychiatric institution? That would mean giving up the attempt to rehabilitate her by medical means. Gail shuddered inwardly, knowing that Bruce would deplore such a move. To Bruce, this would represent a painful failure.

At the same time, there were other patients to

consider. The clinic could offer only limited help from its lone staff psychiatrist. And there was the danger to patients who had a chance at recovery. If Stella was a hopeless paranoid, convinced that she was surrounded by enemies who wanted to murder her, she was capable of injuring, even killing, her imagined adversaries in "self-defense."

Unnerved by the shaking scene, disturbed by this reversal in Stella's progress, Gail managed to take the girl's hand, pressing it between her palms and joining Bruce's litany of reassurances. "You see, Stella? We aren't hurting you. I talked to your father today. He wants to come and see you. I promised him I'd ask you if it was all right. I wouldn't do that if I didn't think you're going to be fine. You're just fine now. Tomorrow you'll feel better. You'll see we were only trying to stop you from running away. You could get hurt, just running out into the street that way. Dr. Cranston doesn't want anything bad to happen to you."

Gail went on in that vein for a long time, keeping her voice calm and soft. Gradually, the sobs were reduced to tired, soundless jerkings of Stella's shoulders. The green eyes, bright with horror a few minutes earlier, took on a glazed, heavy-lidded appearance. Finally, there was silence and Stella closed her eyes, her head dropping downward as the drug took hold of her.

"Will it be all right if I leave, Dr. Cranston?" one of the night-shift nurses asked in a whisper. "I promised Dr. Wibberly I'd get back to Emergency. He has a young man there in this same condition. Bummer LSD trip, as they call it."

Bruce nodded. "Right. Tell Dr. Wibberly I'll be available in a few minutes if he needs my help."

"He will," the nurse said. "Thorazine hasn't helped. This guy's got giant man-eating *pianos* chasing him. Piano keys shaped like teeth. Whew! And he thinks he can escape by flying. His friends grabbed him just as he was going through a fifth-story window at home."

They were all watching Stella De Shiel as they talked, waiting to be sure she was unconscious. "Sounds like fun," Bruce muttered. He was compassionate, but there was disgust in his voice, too. Why, with the medical world plagued by ailments that were *not* self-induced, why in the name of heaven did people deliberately subject themselves to such needless horrors? For a moment's euphoria, for a temporary "kick," for the false promise of deeper insights and an easy way to reach the "cosmic consciousness" for which mystics struggled? What a sham it was! When would they learn that perception and talents were not heightened by the use of drugs? Oh, the illusion of supreme power was often present. The sensation of invincibility, of being capable of glorious achievement, of being in touch with the Infinite.

But the "spiritual" experience, noble as it might appear to the user, was also fraught with danger. How many fine young minds Bruce had seen shattered by a "bummer trip," such as the young man in Emergency was suffering now? Worse still was Bruce's knowledge that the ghastly visions might recur long after the patient had been pulled out of his present state. Weeks, even months later, the distorted phantoms of pianos that snapped at him with ivory teeth might flood his consciousness, as threatening as they appeared now. He might even *know* he was hallucinating, in which case the seeming reality of this would make him question his sanity.

Gail could read Bruce's mind. How many times, after straightening out an emergency patient, had he wondered, angrily, how rational, intelligent young people could fail to realize that drugs were a big money industry and as such had attracted the crime syndicate? They didn't even know what they were taking; certainly the producers didn't care about the purity of the drug or what other poisons they used to extend it, substitute for it. Their object was profit. The price was often, tragically, the destruction of a human mind.

"If Thorazine hasn't done it, the kid may have taken S.T.P.," Bruce was saying now. "Nasty stuff." He stared at Stella for a second longer. "I think we can get her to bed. I want her transferred, though. Do we have another available room in this unit?"

"No empties," one of the nurses replied.

"Then let's make a transfer," Bruce told her. "The Moore boy — where is he?"

"Across the hall. He'll like the change," the nurse said. The orderly had gone to get a gurney on which to move Stella to her new quarters. "He complains about his TV reception."

"Well, they'll both benefit," Bruce said. "I'm not saying Stella's going to feel secure across the hall, but I want her to know we keep our promises." He forced a tired smile. "Among them, her discovery tomorrow morning that she's still very much alive."

Gail helped with the transfer of both patients. The young man named Moore, eager to flick on his new television set, made it under his own power. The nurse who wasn't wanted in Emergency stayed with Stella De Shiel on the slim off chance that the patient might not be completely sedated. ("Gorked" was the term everyone at the clinic used.)

Bruce accompanied Gail as she left Stella's new quarters. "I'd better get over and see how Dr. Wibberly's managing," he said. The latter was a new addition to the resident staff; he would appreciate the help of a more experienced M.D. "Can't say it hasn't been an exciting evening."

Gail released a long sigh. "That really shook me up. She was *so* terrified."

"I wasn't talking about Stella," Bruce said. His gentle expression turned to a concerned scowl. "Hey, that's an ugly scratch. When did that happen? In there?" His nod indicated Stella's former room.

Gail had been too busy to pay attention to the smarting pain. Reminded of it now, her hand went to her neck, coming away faintly red and sticky. "I guess she broke the skin."

"You better believe she did!" Bruce stared at

the scratch, frowning. "You march right over and get that cleaned up and covered."

"I'll do it at home," Gail said.

"You'll do it now before it gets infected," Bruce ordered. "Fingernail scratch on a sensitive spot like your neck. You're going to get a tetanus shot, too, kiddo. And I'd better not find out you left here without it. Have you got that?"

"I read you loud and clear," Gail said. "And if there's one thing I can't stand, it's a bossy doctor who pushes his weight around."

Bruce grinned. "Y'know, I rather enjoy bossing you around. Off duty, I mean. Be fun, finding out whether you're a wildcat, pussycat, or . . ."

"I'm a *tired* cat, right now," Gail cut in. "I'll have surgery before I go home, though."

"Promise," Bruce said firmly.

Gail held up two fingers. "Scout's honor."

"OK. You're dismissed." Bruce said good-night, started down the corridor toward the emergency room, and then turned. His eyes held Gail's for a long moment that encompassed all the thrills she had ever dreamed of knowing. "Take care of yourself, Gail," Bruce said softly. "You could become very precious to me."

Could become. He hadn't said that she *was* precious to him, but the inference had been there. Gail watched until Bruce had rounded the corner at the end of the hall. Then, realizing that the only logical place to get the attention she needed was, at this hour, the emergency room, she traced Bruce's footsteps. Her neck was beginning to hurt now — *really* hurt. But she walked briskly, the disturbing incident in Stella's room swept out of her mind by the memory of a kiss, a word (*"Precious."* *He had said, "Precious!"*), and the thought that she would see Bruce Cranston once more before she faced the long hours before morning when she would see him once again.

Five

Stella appeared too dazed the next morning to notice anything more than the fact that she was "someplace else." This observation was pronounced in a suspicious tone.

If she had any memory of her wild experience the night before, the lovely redhead didn't mention it. Nor did she comment upon, or even seem to notice, the unfortunately obvious square of taped-down gauze on Gail's neck. She seemed to be in a sullen mood, taking the vitamin pill Gail had brought to her with slow reluctance, watching the door warily, but not with panic, during Gail's brief stay in the room.

"Let's see what develops," Bruce had said in answer to Gail's question about whether Stella would remain at the clinic. "Dr. Praeger is going to see her at four today. I'll consult with him later and — let's just say we'll continue our present therapy and see what develops."

Stella had a brief reprieve, then. Gail was cheered by the decision, reporting the encouraging news along with the bad when Charlie De Shiel telephoned later in the morning.

Near the end of their phone conversation, Stella's father asked, "She hasn't said anything about — letting me come and visit?"

"Not yet," Gail told him. "With this setback, I don't want to broach the subject just yet. Please be patient."

"Oh, I don't mean to ask you to do anything that's not right," the voice on the other end of the line protested. "I just mean — well, I know you won't forget. You know how I feel, miss."

"I know. And you keep in mind that Stella doesn't want to see *anybody*. Not just you. Anybody."

"Has she — have there been other people to see her?"

"None that I know of," Gail said. "Not on my shift, anyway." She paused. "I don't think Stella has too many friends."

"And, like they say, with her kind of friends she don't need no enemies," Mr. De Shiel said. He thanked Gail for her "trouble" and said he'd call again the next day. Before he dropped the receiver, Gail told him, "If I'm busy, if you can't reach me or Dr. Cranston, just ask whoever answers for a report. Whoever's at the desk will be able to tell you how Stella's progressing." She was thanked again for that information before Stella's father rang off.

Gail was still behind the counter of the nurses' station writing out a medications report for another patient when Stella De Shiel's friendless state became a thing of the past.

"Excuse me, Nurse," the male voice said.

Gail looked up from the form she was filling out

to see a man who appeared to be in his midthirties. Her immediate impression was one of elegance: a dark suit with an obviously continental cut, shining black hair that had been groomed by an expert stylist. Olive-complected, with sharply chiseled features, the man's face was dominated by black birdlike eyes in which the whites were barely visible. His voice had a raspy, rather intriguing quality.

Gail greeted him, asking if she could help.

"I'm a friend of Miss De Shiel's family," the man said. "Fravel is my name. Louis Fravel."

"I'm afraid Miss De Shiel isn't able to have visitors," Gail told him.

"I understand. My only reason for stopping by was to ask how she's coming along. And to ask if there's anything I can do." Mr. Fravel gave Gail a sorrowful smile. "I know there are heavy expenses, and there's no insurance that I know of."

Gail explained that the clinic was not a private hospital but an experimental venture supported by a foundation and contributions from wealthy benefactors. As such, no patient was refused because of lack of money.

"I see." Mr. Fravel sighed. "I've always been concerned about Stella. She might not even remember me. I've been close to her family since she was just a little girl."

"Then you must have known them when Stella's mother was still alive," Gail said. "What was it Charlie De Shiel told me? She died when Stella was about nine."

"Eight or nine," Mr. Fravel guessed. "It's been a long time."

"Are you from Biloxi?"

"Used to live there. I have my law offices here in the city now. Unfortunately, I was out of town when Stella had her accident. Just learned about it today from my secretary. Good Lord, I feel so sorry for Charlie. I've been trying to reach him by telephone, but I haven't been successful."

"He may have been out on one of his boats," Gail said. "Or is this the shrimp season? I know he calls here every day. He was here yesterday, as a matter of fact."

Mr. Fravel shook his head sympathetically. "How's he taking it?"

Gail related some of her experience with Stella's father.

"Wonderful man, isn't he?" Mr. Fravel ran his hand over his forehead in a distraught gesture. A diamond flashed from a wide gold band on his ring finger. "I must say Charlie was the last man on earth to deserve this."

"Yes, he really loves Stella," Gail said.

"And she's really refused to see him?" Mr. Fravel sounded incredulous.

"She's a very sick girl, Mr. Fravel."

"Is she conscious? My secretary said something about a skull fracture. I wondered if a drug clinic would be equipped to take care of — serious physical injuries."

"We have a staff of M.D.'s," he was informed.

66

"General practitioners plus a consulting staff of specialists."

Mr. Fravel apologized, "I didn't mean to imply negligence. Frankly, I know very little about Stella's injuries. I'm anxious to see that she has whatever care is necessary. Charlie's a proud man. I don't like to embarrass him with the offer of funds, but if there's anything Stella needs, I'd appreciate your getting in contact with me." He reached into an inside jacket pocket for a leather wallet, searched inside one of the folds for a moment, and then said, "I seem to have run out of cards. No matter. I'll have my girl send the information to your billing office. Carte blanche guarantee of financial responsibility if Stella needs any special attention."

"I think the best thing you can do, if you want to help," Gail suggested, "is to make a contribution to the general fund. We treat hundreds of Stellas here, Mr. Fravel. Most of them have no money at all. And no generous friends of the family. Very few are even in touch with their families. That's part of the drug-addiction syndrome."

Mr. Fravel made a deprecating sound. "And to think there are people who make a business of destroying others! Just thinking about it makes my blood boil."

The phone rang and Gail started to answer it when head nurse Debbie Farraday came into the nurses' station saying, "I'll take it, Miss Arnold."

Gail remembered that she hadn't answered the visitor's question about Stella's condition. With

Miss Farraday on hand to take care of the telephone call, she corrected that omission. "There was no skull fracture, Mr. Fravel. Stella was badly bruised, and she'd taken, or been *given,* an overdose of heroin. I'm sure she would have died if she hadn't been found in time. It was a real fluke. Ordinarily, no one would have gone out to that particular alley late in the afternoon."

"Well, we can thank God for that much," Mr. Fravel said.

"Yes. There's nothing wrong physically that won't heal in time. Stella's problem is mental. Paranoiac delusions. Fantasies revolving around — oh, rival gangs, both with motives to murder her."

Mr. Fravel scowled. "You're certain that these are just delusions, miss? I'm an attorney. I've learned not to dismiss even the flimsiest shred of evidence. Stella *was* beaten and left to die, wasn't she?"

"No one's certain. It looked that way."

"What are the police doing about it, for heaven's sake?" Mr. Fravel's obsidian black eyes glowed with resentment. "Has Stella told them what they need to know? Is she well enough to do that?"

"She claims they wouldn't believe her." Gail felt a minor exasperation with this man whose sense of justice evidently demanded instantaneous action. "When you're dealing with a mentally disturbed — *drug* disturbed patient, Mr. Fravel, it's not like dealing with a rational client in a law office. For example, I didn't know whether to believe Stella myself when she told me this dramatic plot. Somebody named Virgil Corbett heading a narcotics ring and a big syndicate deciding to take over the town."

"But, don't you see, miss . . . ?" The attorney hesitated. "I'm sorry I don't know your name."

"Miss Arnold. Gail Arnold."

"Don't you see, Miss Arnold, Stella may be telling the truth! I specialize in corporate law, but on a few occasions, usually as a favor to parents who were friends of mine, I've defended clients who were arrested for possession. For using narcotics. They were victims of the criminals who trade in the horrible stuff. Some were confused, yes. But I'd listen to them, trying to sift fact from fantasy, always trying to find out who supplied them."

"And you probably didn't find out," Gail ventured. "The names of the men at the top, I mean." She smiled. "You couldn't have. I happen to know they're still in operation."

"Oh? Do you?"

"Of course I do. We'd be able to close our doors if they went out of business. And every doctor and every nurse here would be happily unemployed. My point is, Mr. Fravel, that a minor pusher like Stella — an *addict* who couldn't be trusted to secrecy — wouldn't be likely to know the name of the top man she worked for. It's even more unlikely that she'd know who heads the bigger rival syndicate."

"That's true." Mr. Fravel considered the possibilities, probably making a quick analysis in his cagey lawyer's mind. "However, if there's the slimmest possibility, the authorities should be advised. I presume you've told this much to the police, Miss Arnold?"

"I haven't told anyone. Not until just now." Gail motioned to one of the bronze plaques bearing Paul Mascon's name. It hung beside the door leading to Miss Farraday's little office. "That happens to be the name she gave for the head of the syndicate, Mr. Fravel. Mr. Mascon provided the funds to build this entire wing. Now that would be a rather silly tale to bother the police with, wouldn't it?"

Mr. Fravel's thin mouth lifted at one corner in a half-smile. "I'm afraid so. I believe the other man you mentioned — Mr. Corbett — is a prominent businessman, also."

"He owns several nightclubs. Stella probably worked in one as a dancer. And there was a plaque exactly like this one in her room, which made it pretty obvious that she was making her story up as she went along."

"You took the plaque down?" Mr. Fravel asked.

Gail stared at him bewildered. "I don't understand."

"You said there *was* a plaque with Mr. Mascon's name on it in Stella's room. I presume she found it disturbing and it was removed."

Gail shook her head. "I can see that you've been trained to catch details. If I ever need legal help, I'll call on you."

A quick smile of appreciation crossed Louis Fravel's face. "Thank you. I do earn my living by being observant."

"Actually, there's another plaque just like it in her new room. We had to transfer Stella to 109 last night. She was having a serious attack — paranoid delusions. Dr. Cranston promised to move her to a 'safer' place."

"Poor kid." Mr. Fravel repeated his loathing for the ghouls who trafficked in drugs, wrecking the lives of the naïve Stellas of the world. He checked his watch. "I must be going. Thank you, Miss Arnold. I'll be interested in knowing how Stella is getting along. If there's anything I can do."

"I'll tell her you were here, Mr. Fravel."

"If you like. She won't remember me well. Stella was about — oh, twelve when I last saw her, though I've made a few efforts on her behalf since she came to New Orleans. Kept track of her for her father."

"I hope you reach him, Mr. Fravel," Gail said. "If I talk to him, I'll tell him you were here."

"Thank you. I'm sure we'll be in touch. Meanwhile — are flowers permitted? Or would something in the wearing-apparel line be more useful? Does Stella have a robe — slippers?"

"She hasn't shown much interest in anything," Gail said. "But whatever you want to send would be fine. She doesn't have any clothes except what we've been able to provide."

Mr. Fravel nodded as though he had made a decision about what gifts to send. His rather brusque manner of speaking was softened by impeccably polite manners. "I appreciate your time, Miss Arnold." He started to leave the desk, then turned back. "I'm assuming from what you've told me about Stella's condition that she won't be released in the near future."

"Not for a while," Gail reported. "She's far from being well."

"I don't want her returning to her old haunts when she leaves here," Mr. Fravel said. "Same old companions, same old atmosphere. She's going to need a total change." He made an impatient gesture. "I'm being premature. Something I'll have to discuss with her father."

Gail had exchanged good-byes with the visitor while Miss Farraday finished her telephone conversation. As she dropped the receiver, the head nurse scribbled a note, placed it in one of the doctors' correspondence boxes, and asked, "Who was that, Miss Arnold?"

"Man asking about Stella De Shiel," Gail replied. "A friend of her father's."

"I thought it might be someone you knew." Miss Farraday hurried out of the enclosure, leaving the sentence unexplained. Most likely it was a critical remark, implying that Gail had taken too long to tell the man the simple fact that Stella could not have visitors. Annoying, when every nurse knew it was clinic policy to answer the questions of friends and relatives, relieving their worry with honest information about the patient concerned. Miss Farraday had taken to making these petty little remarks lately, reminding Gail of her superior position, demonstrating her perfection.

Hesitant about leaving the desk unattended (Miss Farraday had gone into the room of a patient who was scheduled to be released after lunch), Gail walked over to the telephone. A call to the dispensary would determine how soon nurse June Schuyler would be free to relieve her.

As she reached for the receiver, Gail's glance swept over a note pad next to the instrument. She paused. Miss Farraday had evidently been doodling during that last call; the scratch paper was covered with absentmindedly drawn geometric shapes and tick-tack-toe blanks. What appeared to be a list of names had been scratched out by Miss Farraday's pen, probably the moment they were written down. The names had not been completely obliterated. Gail squinted, then drew a startled breath as she made out the "list." Her superior, who never revealed anything more personal about herself than where she bought her nylon uniforms, had unknowingly recorded a blueprint of her subconscious mind. The names were all one. Or, more accurately, variations on the same theme. The scrawled and pen-marked "list" read:

> Mrs. Cranston
> Dr. and Mrs. B. Cranston
> Debbie Cranston
> Deborah Cranston, R.N.

If ever a woman had been trying on a man's name for size, the secretive head nurse had been doing it! Gail felt a twinge of embarrassment, not unlike being caught peering through someone's keyhole. Except that this was a more intimate prying; it was looking into Debbie Farraday's mind.

It didn't occur to Gail until later that the use of Bruce Cranston's name might not be merely wishful thinking on Miss Farraday's part. Sometime in the past had she been *encouraged* to formulate this daydream? If so, had there been a break with the doctor, perhaps only the temporary interruption of a lovers' quarrel? Was Gail being used to stir up jealousy in the hope of patching up that rift?

No, Bruce was above that. He didn't use people; he carefully avoided anything that would disturb the necessary harmony among members of the staff. Still . . .

Still, a poised, cool, practical woman, one who, before reaching the age of thirty, had reached the top nursing position offered at the Bayou Clinic, wasn't likely to indulge in adolescent fantasies. Miss Farraday had to have some reason, some solid foundation, for practicing a signature that identified her as Dr. Cranston's wife!

Six

Bruce was needed elsewhere during that afternoon period when Gail usually helped him administer methadone to outpatients in the dispensary. She was filing the chart of the last appointee when Dr. Wibberly returned from answering the telephone and said, "Dr. Cranston wants to see you in his office, Gail."

A pang of foreboding raced through her. Bruce had never before summoned her to his office. "Did he say what he wanted?"

The resident shrugged. "That's all he said. 'When Miss Arnold's finished there, would you ask her to come to my office, please.' Period. The end. Go ahead. I can wind up whatever we have to do here."

Minutes later, her apprehension increased by Bruce's unsmiling, formal manner as he asked her to sit down, Gail faced him across the wide desk.

Bruce came directly to the point. "Miss Farraday tells me Stella had a visitor this morning. You hadn't told me."

"There wasn't much to tell," Gail said. She felt relieved; for a while there, she had been afraid that she had made a serious error in medication or neglected to follow an order. "Mr. Fravel

75

didn't *visit* the patient. He only dropped in to ask how she was or if there was anything he could do for her."

"You talked to him quite a while," Bruce said.

Resentment flared inside Gail. "Miss Farraday gave you a very thorough report."

"That's what she's paid to do," Bruce said. There was no rancor in his tone; he had made a simple statement of fact. "So much of our treatment depends upon emotional factors. Friends who care. Lack of friends. The patient's ability to relate to others. This was one of the reasons I valued your report after you'd talked to Mr. De Shiel. We pass this information on to Dr. Praeger. It becomes another weapon in our fight, an adjunct to drug therapy."

"I understand that," Gail protested. "If Mr. Fravel had told me anything of significance, you know I would have passed it on to you. He didn't have any valid information about Stella. He hadn't even seen her since she was — I think he said, twelve. All he did was ask about her."

"What sort of questions?"

"Doctor, I don't understand this — this inference that I've done something wrong. You know the sort of questions a friend of the family would ask. How is she, is everything possible being done for her? Oh — Mr. Fravel *did* say he'd take care of any expenses involved. And he's probably going to send Stella things to wear. *That's* what he asked about."

Bruce was gazing at her with a patient but demanding stare. "Anything else? Please think back."

Thoroughly bewildered by now, Gail dredged her mind, trying to reconstruct her dialogue with the caller. "Let me see. He was somewhat annoyed by the fact that the police weren't doing much. He's an attorney, by the way."

"And you're certain that he's a friend of Stella's? A *real* friend, not one of her recent companions?"

"More a friend of Mr. De Shiel's," Gail said. "He was perfectly honest about that. I mean, he said that Stella might not even remember him, it's been so long since he's seen her. But there's no question that he's close to Stella's father. He referred to him as 'Charlie,' he knew all about Mr. De Shiel's shrimp boats, he knew when Mrs. De Shiel passed away and — and how much Charlie loves his daughter. How proud he is about money. I know that's true. Mr. De Shiel told me he wanted to pay for Stella's care. Even if he had to sell the boats."

Bruce was silent for a moment, evidently weighing Gail's reply. Then he asked, "Are you sure you didn't feed him this information?"

"What?"

"A clever con man, for example, can extract all sorts of personal details from a prospective pigeon. And do it so smoothly the person thinks the information originated with the con man."

"But what reason . . ."

"I'm concerned," Bruce said. "You were tied up

with those two new barbiturate cases we admitted this afternoon. So maybe you don't know Stella tried to throw herself through the window in her room. First floor, she wouldn't have fallen far. But she would have gotten badly cut up if Miss Farraday hadn't acted fast. We aren't going to get far with Stella if we have to keep her gorked half the time."

Gail closed her eyes for a second, visualizing another scene of mindless terror. "What does that have to do with — my answering a visitor's questions?"

"Simply that Stella not only claimed she had never heard of a Mr. Fravel — Miss Farraday caught the name — but she became hysterical with fear when he was described to her."

What else had efficient Miss Farraday been doing besides taking a message for Dr. Roper, overhearing a conversation, and practicing her signature as a married woman? Irritated, Gail snapped, "Stella thinks *you* tried to kill her, too, Doctor. I'm beginning to think we *aren't* equipped to handle Stella's case. Her mind's been destroyed. She's a menace to everyone here, especially to herself."

"I'm beginning to wonder about some things, too," Bruce said. "And I'm not going to see a young patient institutionalized, maybe holed up for life in some damned snake pit, because we weren't intelligent enough to distinguish between a paranoiac fear and terror based on fact."

Gail released an exasperated sigh. "Well, Mr.

Fravel isn't going to qualify as a menace. If you're thinking he's some dope-peddling gangster, I can assure you that he's every bit as incensed about narcotics peddlers as we are. He was even annoyed with me because I haven't reported Stella's story to the police."

"What story?"

"Oh — I made a note of it to give to Dr. Praeger when he comes in. The same sort of ramblings you've heard her make, Doctor. About who's out to get her. You, me, the orderlies, Mr. Mascon."

"Mr. *Mascon?*"

"I'm sure I told you that Stella's built up a fantasy that includes everybody. Including the name she saw on a plaque in her room. According to Stella, Paul Mascon heads the syndicate's narcotics operation in New Orleans."

"You *didn't* tell me that," Bruce accused.

"I — gave you the gist of my talk with Stella." Gail faltered, not certain that she had. "It was the first time Stella opened up and talked to me. In any case, you've heard her repeat the same sort of thing many times. There's a plot to kill her. We're all part of it. Only, Mr. Fravel, being a lawyer and not a psychiatrist, seemed to think I should run to the police with every name Stella mentioned."

Bruce got to his feet in a sudden move that startled Gail. "You told *him* about this conversation with Stella? You told a total stranger and you didn't tell *me?*"

Gail trembled under the irate accusation. "I —

made a record of it. All the names — the so-called heads of two rival gangs Stella thinks are out to get her. Should I have added the names of everybody on our staff?"

"That's enough smart talk," Bruce exploded. Gail had never seen him this furious before; certainly he had never addressed her with such fury. "What I'm gathering — and please correct me if I'm wrong — I'm gathering that you told this man . . ."

"A friend of Mr. De Shiel's."

". . . this total *stranger,* things that, if they happen to be true, could jeopardize Stella's life." Bruce stomped to his window, then whirled around. "And yours, too, come to think of it."

Gail had a momentary sensation of not being sure of herself. Then, her reason dismissing the threat, she said, "I'm beginning to think that paranoia is contagious! Bruce — Dr. Cranston, please think about it! If these — clever criminals were interested in shutting Stella up, they wouldn't have given her time to recover and talk. They would have known where to find her; it was in the paper, the television newscasts. And if the police really thought that the lowest rung on their ladder, an addicted pusher, knew anything worth knowing, wouldn't they have been interviewing Stella?"

"They were here," Bruce reminded.

"Yes, but Stella didn't tell them anything."

"Maybe she *was* afraid."

"She knew they wouldn't take her seriously. Maybe she's at least *that* rational. The names were so obviously picked up at random."

Bruce thought about that for a few seconds. Calmer now, he muttered, "That's true."

"And look. If Mr. Fravel *wasn't* telling the truth, he wouldn't risk coming here and representing himself as a friend of the family, would he? He didn't even ask to see Stella. When I told him she wasn't up to visitors, he didn't insist upon going to her room. Besides, he'd been trying to reach Mr. De Shiel to offer whatever help he could. He's an attorney. She'll need legal advice, once she's recovered. Honestly, he was just doing what any decent friend would have done under the circumstances. And for a reward, he's now a suspected killer. Along with the two of us, I should add. And the businessman who paid for the very furniture in your office. If that isn't galloping paranoia, I don't know what is!"

Bruce gave her a scathing look that told Gail she had gone too far with her argument. "One way to settle this," he said. He lifted the receiver from his phone, drumming the fingers of his free hand against the desk top while he waited for the switchboard operator's response. "Yes, Miss Egers. Would you get the telephone number of a Mr. Charles De Shiel from whoever's at the main-floor station? It should be in the file for a patient named Stella De Shiel. Thank you."

Gail had a brief time to go on explaining her conviction that Stella's terror was imaginary, the result of heroin-induced mental deterioration.

The telephone rang in the middle of her monologue.

"Yes?" Bruce listened for a moment, then said, "Just a minute, please." He turned to Gail. "There's no telephone *or* address for Mr. De Shiel. Don't tell me we didn't get that when he was here?"

Not sure who was responsible for the negligence, Gail said, "We must have forgotten. Asking him everything but where he could be reached!"

Bruce made a disgusted face and addressed the operator again. "I'm sorry, Miss Egers. Would you try to get the number from Information? No, not in the city — Biloxi — That's right. If it's not listed under Charles De Shiel, tell her to check the business listings. The man owns a shrimp boat. He might be listed under some category in that area — Fine — I'll wait."

Another wait, this one longer and made suspensefully endless by Bruce's silence. The switchboard operator reported that there was no listing for anyone named Charles or Charlie De Shiel in the Biloxi area. If he had a business phone, it was not under his own name.

Bruce finished telling Gail the news, adding, "So, if he's been trying to reach Stella's father, Mr. Fravel's performing a neat trick."

"Unless he's calling an unlisted number," Gail said. It was hard to keep smugness out of her voice. "The sort of number only a good *friend* would have."

If he agreed with Gail, Bruce still needed to

save face. This time he literally tore the receiver from its cradle. "Miss Egers, will you try to put me in touch with an attorney here in town. I *believe* he's here in . . ."

Gail nodded from across the desk.

"Yes, he is. Fravel — I'm not sure how it's spelled — yes — it could be E-*double* L-E — Right — Thank you."

Miss Egers called back again in a surprisingly short time, reporting that the only name she had found under Attorneys that might be a possibility was Fraser. There was a listing for Carnes and Fraser, Attorneys at Law, and she had tried ringing their office but had gotten no answer. It was past office hours; should she try again in the morning? Or should the girl who would relieve her keep trying?

"Never mind," Bruce said. "It doesn't sound like the man I'm trying to call." He thanked the operator again for her trouble and turned to Gail. "You're sure this man said his office was here in town? Not in Biloxi?"

"I'm — almost sure," Gail said. "It's so hard to remember every detail. We covered a lot of ground in just a few minutes." She tried to recall her conversation with the man she knew as Louis Fravel, suddenly not sure of anything except that Bruce was making a cloak-and-dagger mystery out of a simple visit. "I can't see what all the fuss is about. The man didn't even particularly want to see Stella. It was a duty call. I told you he doubted that Stella would remember him."

"She remembered him, all right," Bruce said tersely. "Not the name. His description. I had to zap her down with tranquilizers, she remembered him so well."

"She was suspicious when I brought her a vitamin pill this morning," Gail insisted. "Can't you see that she's . . ."

"Will you stop telling me that I'm incapable of recognizing genuine fear when I see it?"

"A paranoid's fear is 'genuine,' " Gail challenged. She had infuriated the doctor, perhaps going too far in suggesting that his distrust was as sick as that of their patient. But her own anger had been roused. "You're acting as though you won't be satisfied unless you prove that I've made a terrible mistake."

"I'm not interested in proving your incompetence!" Bruce yelled. "I'm concerned about what happens to a patient. And if you'd stop thinking you know all the answers, stop acting as though the issue here is your *ego*, we might . . ."

There was a knock on the door, and Bruce stopped his tirade abruptly. He lowered his voice, but it was still loud enough to be heard outside the office. "Come in."

The door opened to admit Miss Farraday. She glanced at Gail, typically cool as she said, "I hope I'm not interrupting something important."

She knows perfectly well what she's interrupting, Gail fumed silently. She got up from her chair, ignoring the head nurse.

"It's all right," Bruce said. "We were about finished."

"Oh. That's good," Miss Farraday said. "I didn't want to rush you, but we're due at the Devereaux's at seven. If we want to grab a bite of dinner first . . ."

Gail caught a glimpse of Bruce checking his watch, then heard him mutter, "We'll have time. But you're right. We'd better be going."

"I instructed Miss Leigh about visitors to Miss De Shiel's room. Dr. Fellman said he'd already conferred with you about special instructions." Miss Farraday sounded like a model of efficiency, which was not unusual. What hurt was knowing she had gotten across to Bruce Cranston that she was doing everything possible to protect a patient. Gail had possibly placed this patient in jeopardy. It was the virtuous heroine pointing up the flaws of the villainess.

Barely able to keep her emotions under control, Gail asked, "Will that be all, Dr. Cranston?" Her voice had a caustic edge.

"I think so. Yes." Bruce sounded noncommittal. He said good-night, then the words were repeated by Debbie Farraday, and Gail was free to leave the office. She pounded down the corridor in a fury, her insides churning, her mind racing with the things she should have said to Miss Farraday.

Alone in her apartment that night, after Gail had tried to ease her restlessness by attempting to locate Stella De Shiel's controversial visitor herself, she began to think of the things she *shouldn't* have said to Bruce Cranston. She had failed to find any attorney named Louis Fravel or anything resembling that name in New Orleans, Biloxi, or any outlying towns near the two cities. What if Bruce was concerned for valid reasons? Even if there were logical explanations for Mr. Fravel's not being listed in the phone books, there was no harm in being cautious. A doctor was responsible; the clinic and everyone who worked there shared his responsibility for the welfare of Stella De Shiel. Wasn't it wiser to be overcautious than to risk *any* carelessness?

It wasn't the issue of Louis Fravel that rankled inside her. If she had made a mistake, it had been an honest one, and Gail stood ready to apologize for it. But it wasn't this blow to her professional pride that kept Gail awake until long past her bedtime. It was jealousy — pure, raw, unadulterated, gnawing jealousy — and the conviction that Bruce had used her to evoke the same emotion in an effort to win back Debbie Farraday after a minor rift. That he had succeeded was all too evident; they had been going out together tonight. Gail had been too upset to notice it at the time, but when Miss Farraday had stepped into Bruce's office to remind him of their date, she had looked positively radiant.

Seven

Although Gail came to work the next morning prepared to apologize for being perhaps too naïve, it was Bruce Cranston who apologized to her.

"A woman phoned just a few minutes after I got in this morning," Bruce said. He had invited Gail to have coffee with him in the doctors' and nurses' lounge, but their time was limited and he spoke rapidly. "She wanted to know what size Stella wore. Fortunately, Miss Farraday took the call and put me on the line. Turned out to be Mr. Fravel's secretary, and when I asked to talk to him, she obliged."

"You *did* talk to him, then? What did you say?" Gail wondered.

Bruce laughed. "It was a little embarrassing. You don't come right out and ask a man if he's a dope-peddling thug or a legitimate lawyer. I must have been fairly cagey. Either that or he realized why we have to be careful. I found out that he confines his practice to a few major corporations. Private clients. So he prefers not to be listed in the phone book. Saves being bothered by people who want a lawyer because their neighbor goofed up their lawn mower and refuses to pay for repairs.

He gave me his office and residence phone numbers and a flock of references. Some fairly prominent people. I felt like a stupid kid who's been playing detective. Building a big case out of nothing."

"You were just being careful," Gail said. "I shouldn't have been so open with a stranger. Even a pleasantly polite one."

"What say we get back to our regular line of work?" Bruce suggested. "I've had enough of this super-sleuth malarkey." He smiled at Gail a bit sheepishly. "I've asked to be called to the phone if and when Mr. De Shiel calls. That should settle the Mr. Fravel thing. I'm sure they're old friends."

If Bruce wasn't ready at that time to admit that Stella's fears were totally irrational, he must have known it later that day. Shortly before he and Gail were due in the dispensary, they were standing before the nurses' station, discussing another patient's case, when Stella had two more visitors.

The couple, who introduced themselves as Mr. and Mrs. Peter Gibbs, were hardly a menacing pair. The husband, a thirtyish man with a doughlike complexion, the drooping features and expression of a St. Bernard, and eyelashes, brows, hair, and moustache that could best be described as colorless, seemed as ill at ease in the smartly modern waiting room as had Charlie De Shiel. He wore a cheap, rather extreme mod slack suit, and when he spoke at all, it was in monosyllables. Awkwardly, he held an oversized bouquet of talisman roses.

Mrs. Gibbs was more articulate. She measured no more than four feet six in her spike-heeled sandals, though her bleached hair was twisted into a high, intricate coiffure that was probably intended to make her look taller. She looked like a vapidly pretty, slightly plump showgirl — which, it developed, she wasn't. For when the doctor asked about her relationship with Stella De Shiel, she said, "I used to be a waitress at The Cinderbox. Stella used to dance there. So we got to be good friends."

Mrs. Gibbs spoke in a shrill and nasal tone, irritating to the ear even though she was aware that it should be subdued because she was in a hospital and was apparently making an effort in that direction. "I really felt awful when I heard about Stella," she said. "I feel like a heel. I didn't send her a card or flowers or nothin'. But I figured at first she'd be too sick to read cards. Know what I mean? I said to Pete, 'Let's wait 'til she's feelin' better and then go cheer her up.' Where's her room?"

Gail exchanged questioning looks with the doctor. "Miss De Shiel hasn't been seeing any visitors," he said testily.

"We'll come back some other time." Mr. Gibbs seemed anxious to leave. His glance darted toward the revolving exit doors. Like so many visitors to whom visiting sick people is an unpleasant duty, he acted as though he had just been given a welcome reprieve.

Strangely, his wife seemed to share this reaction. "I guess — if she's still too sick — yeah. We can't go in her room, huh? Absolutely not allowed?"

"I didn't say that," Bruce corrected. "Miss De Shiel hasn't *wanted* to see any visitors up until now. If you're a close friend, a visit would do her a world of good. Suppose we ask her?"

There was an unaccountable nervousness, as though the couple dreaded a confrontation with a friend who had been exposed as a drug addict. Their behavior was not unusual. Gail had seen close relatives act the same way. What would they say upon meeting the patient? The first meeting under these circumstances was always, if not agonizing, at least embarrassing to the visitors.

"Well, sure," the woman said. "Might as well. If it's allowed, we should go see Stella. That's why we came. Right, Pete?"

Her husband nodded dumbly. Gail reached out for the flowers. "I'll get these into a vase. Do you want me to ask Stella if she's ready for company, Doctor?"

"No, I'll talk to her," Bruce said. He nodded at the couple. "Excuse me a minute, please."

Mr. Gibbs seemed glad to be rid of the bouquet. Gail carried it to a closet several yards down the corridor, filling a vase with water from the sink and hastily arranging the roses. When she was finished, she carried the vase toward Stella De Shiel's room, astounded at seeing that the Gibbs couple, certainly unknown to Bruce, had followed him down the hall.

The door to Stella's room was ajar, and the visitors were waiting outside. There was no sound of voices from inside the room, an indication that Bruce had found his patient either asleep or faking sleep. Mrs. Gibbs gave a vague half-smile as Gail walked toward the door. "The doctor's findin' out if it's OK," she said.

"I think he meant for you to wait in the reception room," Gail said. The couple appeared chagrined by their error, and she softened her tone. "I'll come there and call you if it's all right."

They started back toward the desk, and Gail, using both hands to carry the vase of roses, pushed at the door with her knee.

She had assumed, from the silence, that Stella was not awake. In the next instant, Gail knew that she had been wrong. Either that or the soft bumping sound of her knee against the door had done what Bruce's quiet entrance had failed to do. Stella had responded in her usual manner, jerking to an upright position, her eyes instantly wide open and startled. From her bed, she was able to see the backs of the couple as they moved slowly up the corridor. Suddenly, Stella let out a piercing shriek. Gail nearly dropped the vase in her haste to close the door behind her.

"Don't let them in! Help me! They'll kill me! Oh, Doctor, please — please — call the police! Don't let them kill me!"

It was the same theme all over again, this time triggered by a waitress who had been Stella's friend and the latter's husband!

91

It took all of Bruce's physical strength to keep Stella from leaping out of the bed. The window in her new room was barred by a newly installed iron latticework, placed there not only to give her a sense of safety but to keep her from flinging herself through the glass whenever paranoia overcame her. Thus, there was no place for her to run, except out into the hall.

"You're safe here," Gail said. In her mind, she was debating whether she would be more useful by helping Bruce with his struggle to subdue the hysterical patient, ringing for an orderly (which would mean unlocking the door and adding to Stella's terror), hurrying out to get the hypo that would probably be needed, or using persuasion. Since Bruce hadn't issued an order, she opted for the last course. "I've locked the door from the inside," she told Stella. "There's no way for anyone to get in. Take it easy, Stella. You don't want us to have to give you a shot again. Come on. Pull yourself together."

Perhaps the threat of a hypodermic needle's being stuck into her arm had the desired effect. Stella's shrieks came to an abrupt end. She stopped fighting and sank back against her pillow.

Breathless, Bruce repeated the calming refrain: "It's all right. You're fine. Nothing to worry about, Stella." His expression told Gail that he had given up. The clinic wasn't equipped to handle this case. The barred window had been a concession to Stella's derangement, but it would be impossible to keep her door locked. A mental institution would offer such "protection" to the patient. And other patients in the ward, beset with problems of their own, wouldn't have to endure these frightening eruptions.

As if Bruce needed further convincing, especially since Stella had refused to communicate with Dr. Praeger when the staff psychiatrist had called on her, Stella began to cry. "What's wrong with me?" she sobbed. "That was — a friend of mine. Peggy. She wouldn't — I ought to know better — Peggy wouldn't — hurt me. She was always — at the club — she was always — bringing me stuff backstage. From the — kitchen. Worried 'cause I — didn't eat enough."

"Was she a waitress there?" Bruce asked. Maybe he was only making conversation. Maybe he was still instinctively checking out the story of Stella's visitors, as he had checked Louis Fravel's.

Stella nodded, her face buried in a pillow. "Doctor, what's the matter with me? I'm so — scared! Even scared of — somebody who was — always nice to me."

She dissolved in a fresh flood of tears, and there was no more conversation possible after that. Bruce asked, "Shall we call your friend back, Stella? Would you want her to come in without her husband?" But the only response was an adamant shaking of Stella's head and the muffled words, "I never — knew she — was married."

Confused, afraid, yet lucid enough at intervals to know that her fear was senseless, Stella was in dire need of psychiatric help. Equally fearful of sedation with drugs, she escaped from her torment by keeping her face hidden, sobbing until, a long time afterward, exhaustion overcame her and she fell asleep.

Stella's visitors had evidently given up hope of seeing her. Or they had gotten tired of waiting. When Gail returned to the nurses' station, they were gone.

Between taking care of the outpatients in the dispensary that afternoon, Bruce held a series of conferences with Dr. Fellman, who took over his responsibilities during the next shift. Gail didn't hear what they decided, but she was told the gist of their discussion: Stella De Shiel was not to be exposed to any further visits from friends. Bruce had missed Charlie De Shiel's daily phone call; a new nurse, who had not been instructed to summon Dr. Cranston to the phone, had given Stella's father the routine report on his daughter. "But when he calls tomorrow, I'm going to ask him to come in for a visit," Bruce said. "If Stella refuses to see *him*, we'll know the extent of her illness."

"She might be ashamed. Not afraid, but — ashamed to face her father," Gail suggested.

Bruce had considered that thought. "I know. But she isn't going to go through that horrible fear reaction if he walks into her room. Not if she has any real reasons for being afraid."

"That should settle one problem," Gail said. "You'll be able to ask Mr. De Shiel about Louis Fravel. And — I've been thinking . . ."

"About what?"

94

"About telling the police what Stella told me. I know it's going to sound ridiculous, but I've learned something from you, Doctor."

Bruce had been writing a notation on the last patient's chart. Now he looked up from his desk, his eyes reflecting the same warm interest in Gail that had thrilled her before their rift, before she learned of his association with Miss Farraday. "What have you learned, Miss Arnold?" They invariably addressed each other in a professional manner during working hours, but Bruce had pronounced "Miss Arnold" with more ardor than most men invested in the word "darling."

Bewildered, Gail nearly forgot what she had been saying. She recovered her train of thought. "That even when you think a precaution is silly, if there's just a one-in-a-million possibility that you *could* be wrong, you take steps. I may be wasting my time, the time of some sergeant who'll just put me down as a kook. But I'll feel better if I tell the police about — oh, Stella's fear that the suppliers she worked for are out to get her. Because she knows too much. About the syndicate coming in and offering her a better deal." Gail smiled, sheepish just at the thought of repeating the names of prominent businessmen Stella had named as narcotics kings. "About the big dope-ring bosses."

Bruce agreed that she would probably carry nothing to the authorities but the muddled ravings of a heroin addict in the throes of withdrawal, but he approved Gail's decision. He was so pleased with Gail's about-face that he added, "We ought to go over everything that might possibly offer a clue, even if it's a waste of everyone's time. Go over every word either of us has gotten out of Stella. I'm sure I could contribute some bits that you weren't around to hear. I'll go with you — try to get away during our lunch period tomorrow. All right with you?"

"Fine."

"But we should discuss it first. What about tonight? Any plans for dinner? I'll be busy until seven thirty, but I could pick you up at your place afterward."

"I don't have any other plans," Gail said. She felt a visceral tug. Was Bruce sure *he* didn't have other plans? Was this just another interval between dates with the paragon of perfection he dated on other evenings? She opened her mouth to ask a sarcastic question about Debbie Farraday's plans when their next appointment burst into the dispensary.

"Doc, you won't believe this! Miss Arnold — hey, congratulate me! *I got a gig!* It's just a wedding — only pays ten bucks, non-union, but I got a *gig!* I'm gonna play with this Dixieland combo Saturday night for real money!"

The excited bearer of this good news was, of course, Peter Garvey, the taxicab washer who had been a prominent figure in jazz circles before drug addiction had shattered his career.

"Not enough to quit my job yet, but isn't that something? My clarinet out of hock, a chance to play for an audience again. Oh, man, if it wasn't for you people — if it wasn't for this place, would I be playin' at a wedding Saturday night? I'd be rollin' in the gutter, beggin' for a fix. Or holdin' up some poor Joe who drives a hack. I feel like I'm gonna bawl!"

They all felt as though they wanted to "bawl." Gail remembered Pete's first visit to the clinic, his sickness and despair, his hopelessness as he faced the terrible uncertainty that lay before him. Tears welled in her eyes as another nurse and one of the clinic's orderlies, joined the group gathered to congratulate Pete. They had all played at least a small part in bringing this moment into being. For every failure (and Stella De Shiel would probably fall into that class), for every patient who fell back into the traps of addiction, it took only one ecstatic Pete Garvey to restore their pride in the clinic.

"They won't get any blues out of this baby, no sir! Sock it to me, Doc. Shoot me up with the manna from heaven. Next year at this time, I'll send you all copies of my hit record. You don't think I'll make it? You watch! Long as I've got you people on my side, you watch this baby blow up a storm!"

Bruce listened to the irrepressible enthusiasm, smiling at the excited gestures of the man he had pulled out of an unimaginable hell. His grin broadened as Pete's dream swelled to million-sales golden-hit albums and his own television program, knowing that Pete Garvey was covering his insecurity with bragging exaggerations. Behind Bruce's smile, Gail guessed, was a deep tenderness and a prayer that this patient would never get the idea that he was "cured," that he didn't need the regular injections of methadone, that he could bolster his musicianship with just one little "joy pop" of morphine. Caution, apprehension, touching sentiment, they were all masked by the young doctor's smile. But there was pride, too. Pride and the fondness that develops between doctor and patient when, together, they rout a common enemy.

Bruce faked a punch against Pete's shoulder. "You'll get so rich and famous we'll have to send in a dollar to get your autographed picture," he chided.

"Sure. Yeah, sure. I'll forget your name, Doc." Pete was still smiling, but huge tears were coursing down his face as he rolled up his shirtsleeve. "That'll be the day. The day I forget what you did for me!"

It was past five-thirty before Pete left the clinic to a chorus of "Good luck, fella!", "Play it pretty for the people, now!", and "If they make a tape, bring it in so we can hear you!" Bruce was summoned to Emergency during this noisy farewell, leaving Gail with only the hasty words, "I'll be at your place around eight."

There had been no time, fortunately, for Gail to destroy the magic of an evening with the man she loved by making a jealous reference to Debbie Farraday. Silently, she thanked Pete for the interruption that had stopped her from ruining the evening. Tonight would mean a fresh beginning. Like Peter Garvey, she was determined to make the most of her second chance.

Eight

Gail had nearly reached her little sedan, which waited for her at the far end of the employee's lot, when she saw the man. He had evidently left his car in the adjoining visitors' parking area and was hurrying to the rear door of the clinic, his arms filled with what appeared to be gift-wrapped dress boxes.

Their paths crossed, and she found herself looking at a familiar face. The man appeared to be in a rush, his eyes fixed on a spot behind Gail. She was certain that he would have walked by without glancing in her direction if she hadn't recognized the man instantly and addressed him by name. "Hello, Mr. Fravel."

He stopped short. "Oh. Oh, Miss — Miss Arnold. How are you? Just going off duty?"

"I'm a little late," Gail told him. "We had a small celebration." She nodded at the packages. "Presents for Stella?"

"Yes. I specifically asked my secretary to have the store send these out. She'd just left the office at five, and a delivery boy brought them. Thought I'd run them over. I was passing this neighborhood, anyway."

"I don't think you'll be able to deliver them in

person," Gail said. "Matter of fact, you won't be able to go in through this back entrance."

"I thought I'd leave them with someone at the desk. I don't even know what's inside these boxes. Just told the girl to order the sort of thing a girl could use in a hospital. Dressing gowns; some of those frilly short things they wear."

"Bed jackets?"

"Probably. How do I get around to the front door from here?"

Gail, eager to be on her way, gave him the necessary instructions. Eight o'clock wasn't a long time off when you looked forward to a leisurely bath — time to fix your hair and run an iron over the most flattering dress in your wardrobe.

Mr. Fravel seemed to have more time, now that his fast pace had been interrupted. "I talked to Dr. Cranston on the phone. He told me I shouldn't even try to see Stella."

"No, it's not a good idea."

"So I wasn't planning to. I'll just drop these things off."

"The nurses will see that Stella gets them."

Mr. Fravel scowled. "She's still in bad shape." He made a clucking sound with his tongue. "It's terrible. Poor Charlie's a wreck. I wish there was something I could do for *him*, at least."

"I'm sure just knowing he has friends is good for his morale," Gail said.

"He still hasn't gotten to see the kid."

Gail wasn't sure whether this was a question or a statement. "He hasn't been back since that first visit. But Dr. Cranston's going to ask him to come in next time Mr. De Shiel telephones."

"Good. That's great. I'll do what I can for him. Get him to go to the races with me. Spend a day doing something he enjoys. Get his mind off his troubles." Mr. Fravel repeated the clucking sound. "Such a shame, a fine man like Charlie having to go through all this. I just hope the police get whoever did this to poor Stella. But they're probably dragging their heels, as usual."

Gail was barely listening to the man, her thoughts on the promising evening that lay ahead. Absently, she agreed that the police hadn't come up with any clues. "Maybe they've chalked it up as an accident, though it certainly didn't look like one. I may find out tomorrow when I go to see them. Report what Stella's been telling me."

Gail regretted her disclosure in almost the same instant she made it. Bruce wouldn't have approved, she knew. Still, if Mr. Fravel had heard her, he showed no interest in the fact that she would be going to the authorities the next day with the names of, allegedly, the brains behind two rival drug rings. It had been ridiculous to suspect Mr. Fravel of even the remotest acquaintance with Stella's underground connections.

"Well, I'm not satisfied that everything possible is being done," Mr. Fravel said. "Crime isn't my field, but at times like this, I wish it was. I'd be demanding action. I'm going to do that, anyway." He gestured toward the protruding laboratory wing of the building. "Around there, you say?"

"Yes, there's a sidewalk that'll take you to the front entrance. You can leave your gifts with whoever's at the main desk. They'll be sent back to the intensive care unit."

"Thank you. Nice seeing you again, Miss Arnold."

She responded with similar words, and then Gail was free to hurry home, dismissing Mr. Fravel and Stella from her consciousness while she wondered if the blue knit was worth the time it would take to press it, when the green paisley print was really every bit as pretty and had just been returned from the cleaners.

They had dinner at a favorite spot of Bruce's that specialized in shrimp creole and bouillabaisse. There still wasn't time for the promised meal at Antoine's; that, Bruce said, was for a special evening when he didn't have an appointment with Dr. Praeger at the latter's home — at ten-thirty.

"Praeger's one of the night people," Bruce explained. "His first office appointment is at one in the afternoon. Best time to consult with him, if I don't want constant interruptions, is after ten."

"You're seeing him about Stella?"

"Among other cases," Bruce said. "How's the fish soup?"

"Fabulous. But it tastes better when you call it bouillabaisse."

Bruce laughed. "The chef here once told me he uses thirty-two different ingredients."

"So he wouldn't appreciate your calling it fish soup."

They chatted about a variety of subjects while the meal was consumed. Then, over their coffees, they pieced together fragments of conversations they had had with Stella, Bruce jotting them down in a notebook that he later handed to Gail. "Just in case I'm tied up at noon tomorrow and you have to go alone," he said.

"I hope I have you to give me moral support." Gail glanced over the list of notes and shook her head disparagingly. "I'll feel less absurd if you're there to share the reactions. Now that I look at this, it's more obvious than ever that Stella doesn't need help from the law. She needs Dr. Praeger."

Bruce agreed. Gail hadn't told him yet of her brief encounter with Mr. Fravel. It was somehow an uncomfortable subject, one that would dredge up a reminder that they had gotten into an argument over Gail's last conversation with the man. It was a trivial matter, not worth mentioning. Besides, Bruce had still been in the building at the time; it was possible that he had met Mr. Fravel. Finally, there was Gail's queasy suspicion that she might have again talked too freely to the visitor. Why open up the same unpleasant subject that had created a rift with Bruce once before? She had exchanged a few words of small talk with the attorney. She had told him he couldn't visit Stella, and he hadn't actually intended to do any more than leave his gifts at the desk. Why bring it up?

Why talk about *anything* else when Bruce was saying, "I think we've spent enough conversation on other people's problems, Gail. Can we indulge ourselves for the time that's left? Talk about ourselves?"

"Ourselves?"

"I told you I wanted to think. Make sure of how I feel about you." Bruce's hand reached across the table to take hold of Gail's. "I've had all the time I need. This isn't the setting I had in mind for this, but — I don't want to wait any longer to tell you this."

Gail suddenly felt her heart pounding. It was like knowing exactly what Bruce was going to say, yet being unable to believe it.

"I love you," he said simply. "Love you, need you, want you to marry me. That's not very romantic, honey. It's just — true."

Their eyes met, and then Gail looked downward, concentrating her gaze on the tabletop. She wanted to respond, but no words came to her.

"This is a proposal," Bruce said. "Wrong time, wrong place, maybe. But I'm asking you to marry me, Gail. I'd hoped — I sort of had the idea — that you felt the same way about me. Am I wrong?"

"You're not wrong," Gail said. Her voice was barely stronger than a whisper. "I've loved you for a long time, Bruce. Almost from the first time we met."

"But?"

She was wordless again, unable to express her hesitancy.

"Is something wrong, Gail? You seem to be . . ."

"*Miss Farraday*," she blurted out. "You're being dishonest with one of us. Either Miss Farraday or — me."

Bruce was scowling. "How did *she* get into the act? Honey, you've thrown me a curve I can't begin to understand. What . . . ?"

Now the words, the sentences poured out of her like the flood when a dam bursts. Debbie Farraday's jealous inquiries, the note on which she had practiced signing her name as Bruce's wife, their date together — when was it? Only the night before?

Bruce listened intently, an astounded expression on his face. The bewilderment and shock faded as Gail went on and was replaced by a wide grin of surprise.

"It's not funny!" Gail concluded. "Maybe it is to you, but it's not a bit amusing to me. Or to Miss Farraday, if she's been encouraged to . . ."

"She's been encouraged, all right," Bruce said. Gail had withdrawn her hand from his touch, and now he reached to take it again. "Listen to me, you ninny! Debbie's done something I never thought I'd see. She's pried my cousin Byron loose from his cherished bachelorhood."

"Your . . ."

"My cousin. The dentist. I introduced them some months ago. Two of the most finicky, secretive characters on God's green earth. He hasn't told me they're going to be married. Byron's a great one for formal announcements, proper eti-

106

quette. Miss Farraday — egad, you couldn't get her to tell you what's with her if she found her hair on fire." Bruce covered his eyes with his free hand, laughing silently for a moment. "I gathered it was a serious thing when my cousin invited her to a planning session last night. Mardi Gras Ball planning committee. That's a social affair to which you don't invite anyone outside of your family. And Byron's just enough of a snob to observe that sort of protocol. He's got to be intending to marry the gal. And from the way she was decked out when I drove her to — well, it's the home of *the* society matron in town — Debbie was determined to step into the charmed circle."

Gail felt as though she had been drained. "I thought — I assumed you were —"

"Going out on a *date* with The Silent One?" Bruce laughed again, squeezing Gail's hand. "As Pete says, 'that'll be the day!' Miss Farraday was hesitant about stepping into that spiffy company alone, and Byron was going to be delayed at his office. So I was elected to do the honors. It happened to be on my way home. And Mrs. Devereaux is an old sidekick of my mother's. Gail, honestly, with your imagination, you ought to be writing love confessions!"

Elation mingled with a sinking sensation of having behaved like a fool. "I guess — this is my week to be stupid. I feel as — dumb right now as I'm going to feel tomorrow at noon. I'm sorry, Bruce."

"I'm not," he said fondly. "You were jealous. That's a hopeful sign."

"I'd have sworn Miss *Farraday* was jealous."

"Curious, probably. She's already thinking like a member of the Cranston clan. Look, Gail, do you want the privilege of looking *her* over for approval before she's admitted to the family? Or do you want Mrs. Byron Cranston to decide if *you're* eligible to marry her husband's cousin?"

Gail found herself too overjoyed to do anything but laugh.

"Well, which is it going to be?" Bruce demanded.

Gail returned the warm pressure of his hand. "Me first," she said.

"Then we'd better hurry." Bruce waved for the check. "This isn't any place to kiss you. Let's get out of here. If we're going to set a date, I'd like to have my arms around you while it's happening."

They parked Bruce's car in front of Gail's courtyard apartment, but they didn't set a definite wedding date. Bruce had a ten-thirty appointment, and in the limited time allowed them, there were better things to do than consult a calendar. "Soon" was not quite specific enough, they decided between kisses. "Very soon" sounded much better. For tonight, they let it go at that.

Nine

She was too excited to sleep. The impossible had happened; the daydream had become a reality! She was going to spend the rest of her life with Bruce Cranston, married to the most wonderful man in the world!

Lying in her bed, trying to recall every precious moment of the evening and savoring every word that Bruce had said to her, Gail was startled by the ringing of the door chimes. Her alarm clock read eleven twenty-two. That meant it could only be Bruce.

Finished with the meeting with Dr. Praeger, he had probably decided to come here, as eager to spend every possible moment with Gail as she was eager to be with him.

A robe thrown hastily over her pajamas, Gail opened the door, ready to greet Bruce with a welcoming embrace. She caught a startled breath at the sight of two men, both of them massive, both of them grim-faced.

Gail's first instinct was to slam the door and lock it. Then the older of the two men opened his suit jacket to flash a silver badge. "I'm Sergeant Russo, narcotics division. This is my partner, Officer Hart."

Gail released her suspended breath. Her legs had started quaking under her.

"Sorry to disturb you, Miss Arnold. We'd like to talk to you."

Gail recovered her composure and ushered the detectives into her living room.

Neither of the men sat down. The black-haired man who had introduced himself as Sergeant Russo had small, piggish eyes with which he inspected the room with one sweeping glance. He had the dark-shadowed cheeks and jaws of a man who looks unshaved minutes after he has run a razor over his face.

His partner, who had removed a lightweight fedora hat to reveal a bald, bullet-shaped head, walked around the room, apparently accustomed to surveying every detail. Gail noticed that he had a habit of flicking his right thumbnail against the side of his forefinger, punctuating his steps with the clicking noise.

Their silent appraisal of the room revived Gail's nervousness. "I was going to come to talk to someone at the police station tomorrow," she said.

"We know," Sergeant Russo said tersely.

"You know?" Gail thought for a second. "Oh. I guess Dr. Cranston called to make an appointment."

"Cranston," the sergeant repeated. "He's at the clinic?"

"Yes. What — what is it I can tell you?"

"We want you to tell the bureau chief," the bald man said. He nodded at his partner. "Sergeant

Russo can tell you our plan."

"The narcotics division has been working on this case for a long time," the man with the dark facial stubble said. "We could have cracked down a long time ago, but all we'd of gotten in our net was the small fish. We hear Stella De Shiel told you who the big operators are."

Gail felt a glow of importance. "I thought she was just imagining things. She's very sick, you know. If I had thought she was telling me the truth, I'd have come to you right away."

"Better late than never, miss." The bullet-domed man followed his statement with an audible click of his thumbnail.

"Well, if — if you'll sit down, I'll tell you as much as I remember," Gail offered. "I know that . . ."

"We want you to tell the chief," Sergeant Russo cut in. "And we want you to identify somebody for us. Ever see a short, kind of good-looking peroxide blonde around the hospital? Friend of Stella's?"

"You must mean Mrs. Gibbs." Gail described the couple who had caused Stella's last spell of hysterics.

"Sounds like you've met the party we're talking about," the sergeant mumbled. "If you'll get dressed, we'd like to drive you over to where this — 'Mrs. Gibbs' works."

"Isn't that her name?" Gail asked.

Sergeant Russo shook his head to imply that it certainly wasn't. "Could we get going, Miss Arnold? We want to run you over to see the chief after you peg this — woman. We've got a lot of calls to make before the night's . . ."

His words were stopped by a shrill ring from the telephone. Officer Hart moved toward the instrument, then paused. It rang again as he looked to his superior for instructions. Gail had already crossed the room to answer the phone.

"Don't tell anyone we're here," the dark-haired detective instructed. "Pretend you're alone."

"But, why should . . . ?"

"I'll explain later," Gail was told. "This is a risky matter. We don't want to let anyone know what we're doing."

Gail looked at him, puzzled, then lifted the receiver as the phone was ringing for the third time. "Hello?"

"Gail?" It was Bruce's voice. "I'm calling from the clinic." His next sentence had the effect of a thunderbolt piercing her consciousness. "We've lost Stella De Shiel, honey. She's dead."

Stunned, Gail listened to the incredible report. Bruce had been summoned from his meeting with the psychiatrist by Dr. Fellman. When the patient could not be aroused for dinner at six thirty, the night staff had made an all-out effort to revive her. They had failed. By the time Bruce Cranston had been reached, Stella was in a coma as deep as the one in which she had been found after her beating or accident. Bruce had rushed to the clinic, arriving minutes after the patient had expired.

"But why?" Gail asked. She was aware of the intense stares of the two detectives standing beside her. "What was it?"

"We're trying to locate Mr. De Shiel now," Bruce said, "to get his permission for a post. Without an autopsy, we can't be absolutely certain. But what we've gotten from the lab so far — and from a fresh needle mark on her neck, we're almost positive. Stella was killed by a massive dose of heroin."

Gail sucked in her breath. "But that's impossible!"

"I would have thought so, too," Bruce said in a grim tone. "Until one of the nurses told me she'd seen a visitor coming out of Stella's room. All the nurses were busy with early-dinner trays. Right after the shift changed. She didn't think anything of it, she told me, because the patient wasn't making her usual fuss about visitors. Besides, she assumed the head nurse had OK'd the visit. Trouble was, the head nurse was with me. Admitting a badly shaken youngster on a bad LSD trip. The desk was deserted for about ten minutes. And the nurse barely glanced at the man. Figured he might be one of Stella's relatives. Damn it, Gail, what was wrong with me? Why didn't I give Stella the protection she begged for? My conscience is killing me."

"The man . . ." Gail faltered. "Did she describe him at all? Did she tell you . . ."

"Sleek black hair. Rather short. That's the only impression she got." Bruce hesitated for an instant. Gail saw the detectives move closer to her,

113

intent on trying to catch the other half of the conversation. "Oh, yes . . . she noticed the man was exceptionally well-dressed and was I carrying several gift-wrapped boxes."

"Carrying them *out* of the room?"

"He didn't leave any clue to go on, if that's what you mean. The packages were apparently just a dodge — an excuse in case he got caught sneaking into the room. Stella must have been dozing when he came in. No one heard any outcry from her. But — the reason I'm calling, Gail — the police have been here. Two are actually still here. I gave the sergeant your home address, so you'll probably be getting visitors. They know you can supply details they need. I thought you'd like to be prepared."

"They . . ." Gail paused, remembering that she had been told not to mention the detectives' presence. Still, it seemed absurd not to tell Bruce that the police had already called on her. Without knowing why, she camouflaged her reply. *"That condition exists,"* she said.

Bruce sounded puzzled. "They're there now?"

"That's right."

"Gail? Is everything all right? Listen, I'll call you back. They're paging me — maybe they've reached Mr. De Shiel. Anyway, the coroner just came in. I'll give you a ring just as soon as I can get away."

"Bruce . . ."

It was too late. He had said a hasty good-bye adding, "I love you," and dropped the receiver.

For a moment, Gail stood motionless, frozen in position with the telephone pressed against her ear, palpably conscious of the demanding stares of the two men at her side. Suddenly, a fragment of conversation with Charlie De Shiel, then another seemingly casual statement from Louis Fravel, clashed together in her memory, flooding her with a nauseating fear. She connected the fragmentary bits of dialogue now: Stella's father attempting to convince her that he had set his daughter a flawless moral example. He didn't smoke, he didn't drink, he didn't chase women, *he never gambled.* Then, Louis Fravel (if that was really his name) saying, *"I'll do what I can for him. Get him to go to the races with me. Spend a day doing something he enjoys."* Mr. Fravel didn't know Charlie De Shiel! He was no friend of the family! But Stella had known him. Her terror at hearing his description had been justified!

Gail was still holding the telephone, although the hum of an open line could probably be heard by the detectives. Another thought had immobilized her: The man named Louis Fravel had murdered one person. He knew that Gail had the same information. And he knew that she had intended to carry her story to the police the next day. What if the two men who had closed in on her now weren't detectives at all? *What if they had been sent by the same authority who had directed Fravel to silence Stella?*

Her fear subsided. Bruce had sent them. They were here to investigate Stella's death. Gail muttered "Good-bye," to the empty line and lowered the receiver. "You didn't tell me," she said quietly, "— you didn't explain that you're here because Stella De Shiel's been murdered."

There was a brief electric silence. Then the sergeant asked, "Who was that, miss?"

"Dr. Cranston. He said — from the only eyewitness they have — it was probably a man named — at least, that's the name he gave me — Louis Fravel."

"Fravel." Officer Hart rolled the name over his tongue as though trying to place it in his memory.

His partner was quicker. "He uses a lot of names. Don't worry about *him*. We've already got him in — custody."

Was the other man's smirking reaction only imaginary? Gail wasn't given time to ponder the matter. "How soon can you be ready to leave?" Sergeant Russo asked.

"Leave?" Gail's intuitive uneasiness had returned. "Couldn't I answer your questions here?"

"You can't identify a suspect we're interested in here," she was told. "We're taking you to a place called The Cinderbox. After that, the chief wants to see you. He's a busy man, miss." The face that looked unshaved in spite of its smoothness lit up in a faint, quickly passing smile. "Does the top doctor at your hospital make house calls?"

Gail felt reassured again. The confidence and queasiness took turns inside her while she dressed in her bedroom. If these men weren't narcotics officers, if their intention was to silence her, they would have done it immediately. She reminded herself over and over that her instinctive dislike of the two men was immaterial. They were engaged in a tough job; she couldn't expect them to have the genteel manners of the men she worked with. Besides, Bruce had given them her address. Hadn't he? *Hadn't he?*

Gail's tremulous feeling passed when the unmarked black Cadillac deposited them at a raucously noisy "topless" bar in a street lined with equally uninviting, sleazy night clubs. This was where Stella had launched her dream of a glittery career, a dream that had ended tonight in her murder. The detectives were tight-lipped, scanning the clientele with practiced eyes but more interested in the employees. They sat at a crowded corner table, waiting for a waitress to notice them. Through the thick blue haze of smoke, Gail watched the degrading gyrations of a girl who could have been Stella De Shiel except for the more flamboyant shade of her red hair. The glaring spotlights that illuminated her performance seemed to be the only lights in the crowded, airless room.

They had been in the club for perhaps five minutes when a shadowy shape carrying a tray of cocktails emerged from the semidarkness. Over the thumping of drums, Gail heard a familiar nasal voice say, "I'll get your order in a second, folks."

Gail looked up, peering through the haze at the waitress's face. Apparently the woman saw Gail and the two men flanking her at the table in the same instant. She made a thin, whining sound, expressing shock. Then, Stella's "friend," who had called herself "Mrs. Gibbs" at the clinic, lifted one hand to her mouth as if to suppress a scream. The tray tilted in her other hand, the cocktail glasses sloshing their contents as they slid to the edge, one of them crashing to the floor. Even in the dim light, the horror in the woman's eyes was inescapable. Her face was drained of color.

Neither of the detectives said a word. Gail wasn't looking at them, but she could sense their steely-eyed gaze as the blonde waitress slid the tray onto a tiny table at her side, whirled around, and half-ran, half-stumbled toward a door next to the bar, picking her way between the jammed tables and chairs like a broken field runner at some deadly football game.

Sergeant Russo waited until the waitress had disappeared from sight. Then, turning to Gail, he asked, "Ever see her before?"

Gail nodded and told him of the circumstances. She described the waitress's visit to the clinic and Stella's varied reactions while the sergeant extracted a wallet from his pocket, tossing a ten-dollar bill on the table in a contemptuous manner. Maybe the club had a cover charge; the money wasn't necessary to cover the cost of drinks, for they had ordered none.

"Stella's first instinct must have been right," Gail concluded. Her brain swam; nothing was what it seemed to be. Had the blonde and her alleged husband been sent to kill Stella? Failing, had Louis Fravel been sent in their stead? Her shock at seeing that the law was on her trail was obvious. "Mrs. Gibbs" was probably making a futile attempt to escape. Gail suspected that the rear door of the club was covered by other officers. Whatever her part in the tragedy of Stella De Shiel, the diminutive blonde had reached the end of her trail. Her behavior had revealed that she knew it.

There was a pushing back of chairs as the two detectives got to their feet wearily. This was an old routine for them, Gail guessed. There was an almost bored quality to the sergeant's tone as he grumbled, "Let's get going."

Ten

Gail's apprehension returned during the long drive to wherever she was to meet the chief of the narcotics bureau. To begin with, wedged between the bald man who was at the wheel and the dark stubble-faced sergeant, Gail was made uncomfortable by the almost eerie silence. The two men answered her few questions with grunts or monosyllables. There was no longer the slightest effort at affable manners. There was something purposeful and grim about their lack of communication with Gail or, for that matter, with each other.

As the Cadillac purred beyond the city limits, and houses, lights, and other signs of habitation became more sparse, Gail heard her voice quaver as she asked, "Where are we going?"

"The chief wants to see you," was the terse reply from the driver.

"I thought — he'd be at police headquarters."

"We work under cover," the man at Gail's left muttered. As though he'd had enough of the conversation, he reached out to flick on the car's radio. Rock music filled the air. The fast-paced rhythm was accented by the driver; guiding the car with his left hand, he kept time with the music with that irritating flick of his thumbnail against his other fingers.

Once, as they traversed a dark road that appeared to be banked on either side by a reed-covered swamp, Gail thought she heard the melancholy sound of a steamer whistle. Were they near the docks? She was too unfamiliar with the area to orient herself. All she knew was that with each mile, with every turn in the road separating her farther from the city, her breath became shorter, her heart beat more rapidly. Her mouth felt parched. She had the feeling that if she asked any further questions now, she would get no reply at all.

At the hour, the rock music was replaced by a five-minute newscast. After a capsule coverage of worldwide news events, the announcer read a report on the mysterious death of Stella De Shiel, a patient at the Bayou Clinic, a death that was tentatively listed as murder by the forced injection of heroin. Gail listened, her breath suspended. The men at her side remained silent, expressionless, as the voice went on:

"A city-wide search for the prime suspect has failed to reveal the whereabouts of a recently disbarred attorney who was last seen leaving the victim's room. Known by a variety of aliases, including James Fravelli, Louis LaFollette, James Fravel, and Lou Fravel, the suspect is known to have connections with criminal elements in this city and San Francisco, and was at one time the

attorney for hoodlum Gary Larrimer in a depor-tation case after the latter's arrest on charges of importing narcotics into . . ."

Sergeant Russo's hand shot out swiftly to si-lence the radio. The fury of the motion was like a knifethrust to Gail's midsection. *These were not po-lice officers! They were no more detectives than "Louis Fravel" had been a friend of the De Shiels'!* Fear, acrid in her mouth, strained her words. "You — you told me the police had the suspect in custody. The announcer just said . . ."

"He's in custody," the bald driver said flatly.

No more was said until after the car had turned off the paved highway onto a long, winding stretch of gravel road. The trail (for it was barely wide enough for two cars to pass each other) bi-sected an expanse that resembled the swampland in its flatness and desolation, but here and there the car's headlights caught the outline of pal-mettos growing near the roadside. There were no lights visible in any direction. A wind had risen; warm, humid air added to Gail's feeling of suffo-cation.

They had driven along the secluded road for perhaps twenty minutes when several pale squares of light indicated that they might be approaching their destination. Rigid with fear, Gail tried to voice a question. Her throat was paralyzed; no words emerged.

The Cadillac came to a stop before a huge, two-story frame house, probably an antebellum relic.

It may have at one time been the handsome manse from which a plantation was over-seed. A yellow light illuminated a small expanse of the portico, outlining mammoth columns from which the white paint had been eroded in spots. A dead tree, its grotesque branches festooned with Spanish moss, and a few scraggly magnolia bushes were the last vestiges of what had probably been a formal garden long ago. Three or four late-model cars flashed under the lightbeams thrown by the Cadillac. A single lamp glowed inside the lower level of the house. More lights burned on the second floor.

Once, after she had gotten out of the car and was being escorted to the weatherbeaten front door, Gail hesitated, the tremor in her voice revealing her fright, "I don't think I . . ."

"The chief's waiting upstairs." Gail was too close to releasing her suppressed terror in a scream to know which of the two men had spoken to her.

A musty smell pervaded Gail's senses as the door was unlocked and pushed open. The single unshaded light bulb barely illuminated a vast room that was apparently being used as a warehouse. Except for a badly chipped marble fireplace, there was nothing in the room but a few stacks of wooden shipping cartons. To the left of this gloomy room, parallel with the door, a wide stairway swept upward. Its protective railing, made of grape-patterned wrought iron, had once been painted white. Now the dusty gray swirls of metal had a chilling effect, something hard and cold to the touch that belonged to another time. The railing flashed a remembrance of an historic graveyard Gail had visited with her aunt during that half-remembered childhood vacation. She shuddered, wishing there was someplace to run. Bolt out the door? Where would she go? Where would she hide in the windswept desolation outside?

Gail climbed the stairway, one of the men preceding her, the other following. Predictably, the wooden steps creaked under their weight. She was biting her lower lip to keep herself under control when they reached the second-story landing. They walked down an ecru-painted hallway, barren of any decorations except a darkened gilt dado and lighter-colored rectangles where paintings had apparently once been hung. The moist smell of decay was omnipresent.

A door at the end of the hallway stood open. Several men, as immaculately attired as the two who accompanied Gail, waited in the doorway; they had undoubtedly watched the Cadillac's arrival and were waiting for the newcomers.

There were guttural sounds that passed for greetings. The lack of communication added to Gail's sensation of being among aliens from another planet. How did you reason with men whose faces revealed no emotion, whose rare words had the sound of animal grunts?

As Gail and her escorts approached, the other men stepped aside to let them enter. Gail felt herself being inspected with cool detachment. *Reptilian detachment?* No one had introduced her, greeted her, even acknowledged her existence, except for unsmiling stares that could have as easily been directed at a scurrying insect.

Her nerves and muscles had tightened; it was difficult to walk. Yet somehow she was in a wooden-floored room, sparsely furnished with several new-looking canvas folding chairs and a collapsible metal table. Seated behind the table was a man who looked completely out of place in those shabby surroundings.

Even if he stood up, Gail suspected, the man would appear small. He had a refined, delicate face, brown hair distinguished by a sprinkling of gray at the temples. His blue eyes, which smiled at Gail from behind steel-rimmed glasses, had the effect of making her wonder why she was unable to draw a full breath. Dressed in a conservative gray suit, white shirt, and dark tie, the man whose presence behind the folding table gave it an aura of an executive desk, hardly needed the last convincing note of respectability that set him apart from the others in the room; in his lapel button was the insignia of a well-known service club known for its charitable activities.

Gail was staring at the man, almost certain that she had seen that pleasant face somewhere before, when she saw him smile. Then she heard him say, "How are you, Miss Arnold? Won't you sit down?" A small, well-manicured hand motioned at one of the folding chairs.

Gail sank into it, still tense but glad to get off her feet; her legs had been threatening to buckle under her.

The man, whose diminutive stature in no way reduced his look of authority, turned his smile from her and gave a discreet nod to the others in the room. Almost as though he had waved a magic wand, the men disappeared. There was only a brief shuffling of feet on the grimy wooden floor, then the closing of a door behind Gail's back. She was alone with the "chief," whoever he might be.

He told her in the next instant. "I'm Inspector Carstairs, Miss Arnold. Sorry about the — unconventional time and place. Perhaps my men told you that we're obliged to work under a cloak of secrecy. I felt it was more — prudent to meet you here rather than risk having it known that you gave out pertinent information at a police station."

Incredible! She had been scared senseless a moment before! The inspector, whose almost feminine bone structure belied a powerful, yet engaging personality, had lowered his voice. He sounded and now looked like the affable but still practical loan officer at a banking institution. "We don't have much time, Miss Arnold. Suppose we get right down to cases? It's my understanding that a patient of yours, the same Miss — what was her name?"

"De Shiel," Gail said.

"Yes, that's it. Miss De Shiel, who — I expect

you know that she passed away this evening under circumstances that merit investigation?"

Gail nodded. "I heard that."

"Yes. Well." The narcotics bureau chief cleared his throat. "I understand that Miss De Shiel gave you information that you believe would be of value to us in our crackdown on illicit drug traffic coming through the port of New Orleans. What, precisely, were you told, Miss Arnold?"

Gail repeated the story, believing it now — ironically believing every word, now that it was too late to help Stella. Her fury with the vultures who traded on human misery punctuated her recitation. When she had exhausted her memory, she fished out the list of notes Bruce had made for her during dinner that evening, adding his remembrances of conversations with Stella De Shiel to her own.

Inspector Carstairs jotted the information into a notebook, evidently considering Gail's testimony worthy of his personal attention. When he had completed the list of names, he glanced upward, peering over his glasses. "You say someone else heard Miss De Shiel say the syndicate was out to silence her. Who was that, Miss Arnold?"

"Dr. Cranston. I work with him at the clinic."

"Full name?"

"Bruce Cranston."

The information was duly recorded. Gail's earlier fears had been replaced by a sense of civic importance. She was making a valuable contribution to a roundup of heinous criminals who created human wreckage like Stella. Smash them and the clinic would no longer be necessary. Gail experienced a glow of heroic virtue. She was playing a major part in a vital undercover operation.

"I think that's it." The inspector snapped his notebook shut. "I want to thank you, Miss Arnold. We may have to call on you again. We'll be contacting Dr. Cranston. I'll see that my men get you home." He rose to his feet, and Gail imitated his move, discovering that she towered over the chief by at least two inches.

He was crossing the room, apparently intending to summon the taciturn detectives who had brought Gail to the abandoned house. He was several feet away from the door when it was abruptly opened.

"Paul — the guy's dead!"

Two of the men Gail had seen earlier had burst into the room. In contrast with their earlier nonchalance, they appeared agitated.

Their chief's eyes narrowed. "What do you mean, he's dead?" He shot a wary glance in Gail's direction. "I thought I told you to stay out of here."

"It don't make no difference if she knows, boss." This came from one of the hoods (and there was no other way to describe the man who thumbed in Gail's direction, barely looking at her). "Listen, Paul, how did we know the fink was gonna konk out on us? We worked him over like you said."

The thug's companion, a surly-looking gorilla

of a creature, joined the frantic explanation. "We were gonna drag it out. Like you wanted, we got a tape recorder goin' — so you could play it for the punks he was workin' for. Let 'em know what happens to anybody what don't get outta your way."

"The guy was screamin' his head off," the other man said. "All of a sudden — zam! He's deader'n a dodo."

Gail stared, horrified at the change in the personable man she had been talking to. "Inspector Carstairs" — or Paul — Paul *Mascon?* — was furious. The gentle blue eyes had become glittering darts of fury. "I told you to make it *last!* Damn double-crossing little mouthpiece. I wanted him to pay his dues." He turned abruptly to Gail, his manner less suave now. He shrugged his shoulders in a resigned gesture. "All right, you know. I was going to spare you any unnecessary — qualms. These idiots blew it." It was like witnessing a revolutionary change in someone's character, like being, suddenly, in the presence of someone you had never seen before.

"*Paul.*" One of his underlings had called the little dictator "*Paul.*" Gail felt close to fainting. *Was that why he looked familiar? Hadn't she seen his picture in the newspaper not long ago? Paul Mascon? Realtor, insurance broker, head of a major savings and loan association, heading up an important fund-raising drive for a well-known charity! Stella hadn't learned the name from a commemorative bronze plaque at the clinic! She had known Paul Mascon was head of the syndicate's narcotics operation in this city! Only minutes earlier, Gail had let him know that she was aware of this fact, too. What had made her think he was going to let her go? And now, completely exposed, what hope was there that he would let her live?*

The spectacled blue eyes flashed their venom at the two hirelings. "OK, get rid of — whatever's left of him. And this time don't bungle the job!" The men started to leave but stopped as "Paul" signaled them to stop. "Wait a minute." He sounded now as friendly and reasonable as a compassionate father. "I'm sorry, Miss Arnold. I thought I'd go easy on you. After all, you didn't get involved in this picture intentionally."

Gail's fingernails dug into her palms. "Can't you just let me go? I told you what you wanted to know. I'll forget I ever . . ."

"Unfortunately, I have too much at stake to accept that premise. You see, my dear, I *am* Paul Mascon. And your knowledge *could* prove embarrassing to me." He was actually sounding as though he felt sorry for her. "I thought it was contemptible of Fravel. When he saw which way the wind was blowing, he offered to sell me your name. He had orders to shut up the De Shiel woman from my . . ." An ironic smile flicked across the speaker's face. "From my would-be competitors. He hired a minor pusher who botched the job. Stupid waitress. I've decided *she* may know more than is good for her health. Appreciate your identifying her for us, Miss Arnold."

"I don't know any more than I've told you." Tears sprung up in Gail's eyes. "Please. I don't want to get mixed up in . . ."

"Unfortunately, dear, you have *gotten* involved," Paul Mascon said. He spoke in a subdued tone, almost paternally gentle. "This was why I wanted to handle the matter in a civilized way." He glared at the room's other occupants. "Before these brainless wonders broke in and opened their stupid mouths."

There was no protest from Mr. Mascon's underlings. Huge, menacingly ugly men, they accepted the insults from this little dictator in sheepish silence. It gave Gail a clue to the man's power. As the truth flooded over her, the horrible realization that she had stepped into a trap from which she would not emerge alive, Gail pressed the back of her wrist over her mouth, too numbed to cry, aware that no amount of pleading would alter Paul Mascon's plans. He was only concerned with the degree of her suffering before she died!

"I told you morons that I wanted this one disposed of fast and easy." He glowered at the other two men. "She wouldn't have known what hit her." He turned to Gail, astoundingly calm and reasonable, almost apologetic. "I have a daughter approximately your age, Miss Arnold. I intensely dislike the position you've placed me in. For a man in my situation — certainly you can understand."

Gail started to voice a protest, but all that

131

emerged was a broken cry: *"Please . . ."*

"That double-crossing swine downstairs, that's another matter," Paul Mascon went on. "Trying to play both sides. Crossing his own outfit. For all I know, playing footsie with the cops, too. We waited until he took care of the De Shiel woman. Saved us that trouble. Then instead of paying him to find out who else knew my name, we picked him up. It didn't take my boys long to get the information out of that little weasel."

"Boss, what do we do with what's left?" one of the hoodlums asked.

"Same place. This time use enough lime." Paul Mascon jerked his head in Gail's direction. "Take her downstairs. Wait until I'm gone before you do the job." He muttered the final words to himself: "I'm sensitive."

Gail had started to sob. Now, as the two men moved toward her, she cried out, "No! Please don't! I won't tell anyone what — I —"

"We have to be sure," she heard Mascon purring. "Hurry up, you goons! This sort of thing unnerves me."

Gail screamed as her arms were grasped and twisted behind her. One of the men was holding her wrists in an iron grip. The other, placing a hand on her throat, pushed his inhuman face close to hers, leering, "This one would have been fun to work over."

Paul Mascon moved with the swiftness of a cobra. He had to reach upward to bring his small hand across the man's face in a resounding slap.

"I told you fast and easy, Turk! Now cut out the smart talk and get going."

Gail's cries went unheard as the man touched his fingers to his face; it had been a full-swinging blow. But he accepted this, too, without a word. Grabbing Gail's left forearm, he started pulling her toward the door, his partner forcing her forward. Struggling only increased the pain in her shoulder. *This couldn't be happening! They were going to kill her! In a few minutes she would be dead, and there was nothing she could say, nothing she could do to save herself! These were the heartless machines Stella had feared. She had known that when they decided to kill you, nothing would stop them!*

Sobbing convulsively, Gail went limp, too agonized to struggle any longer. She felt close to fainting as she was half-pushed, half-dragged to the door. They were almost in the hallway when Paul Mascon stopped them with a sharp outcry. "Hold it! There's someone here!"

The man who had been pulling her dropped his hold on Gail's arm, making quick steps across the room. The other, still pinning Gail's arms behind her, made a sudden turn that sent a shock of pain through her. She could see Mascon and his hired thug at the window now. The roar of several motors reached her ears.

"We're expectin' Whitey," the hood said. "Some of the boys . . ."

"That's not Whitey's car." Mascon peered outside. "There's two — no, there's another one coming up the road."

"The cops! It's a raid!"

"Those aren't cops, you damned fool! They're getting out — that's a shotgun the first guy —"

"They wouldn' have the guts to —"

"They were crazy enough to try buckin' the syndicate. Where in hell are the boys? Get downstairs, quick! Give them a dose of lead before they . . ." Paul Mascon looked openly terrified now. *"Get down there!"* he shrieked. *"You — Pony — move!"*

The man who was holding Gail hesitated. "What about the broad?"

"Leave her up here. I'll stay here and . . ."

A rattle of what must have been machine-gun fire ripped the air. Gail was thrust forward, tumbling and falling as she was hurled back into the room. She caught a glimpse of her two captors, guns drawn, racing into the hall. Then the pounding of footsteps, agitated yells from downstairs, and the loud cracking of gunfire. Down below, the noise resembled that of a battlefield.

The new arrivals were no saviors; Gail had as much to fear from them as from Paul Mascon and his cold-blooded hoodlums. Still there was this distraction, this providential delay in her execution. A renewed spirit of resistance came over Gail, a determination to somehow survive. A few seconds ago the odds had been hopelessly stacked against her. Now she had only one adversary to overcome. A small effete man. If the outwardly respectable head of the narcotics ring was unarmed, there was a chance. Part of Gail's training at the clinic had covered self-protection in the event that a drug-crazed patient attacked her. She had been given a rudimentary course in karate. Overcome Mascon? Escape through some back door, hide until the gang war that was in progress downstairs had ended? Stay hidden — somewhere out there in the fields of palmettos and brush?

It was a chance, her only one. Gail dragged herself up to her feet, her mind racing, wondering if her nerve would desert her before she made the necessary lunge at the solicitous little man who was too "sensitive" to hear the gunshot that would kill her!

On her feet, Gail turned around, expecting to find herself looking at a pointed gun. Instead, she sucked in a sharp breath.

Paul Mascon was crumpled on the broad windowsill, a pool of blood forming on the floor below. There had been no outcry of pain, no thud of his body falling. If there had been, the din of gunfire from the lower story had drowned it out. He was sprawled on the wide ledge in a grotesque position, arms and legs askew. But he was not motionless. As Gail stared at him, unable to believe what she was seeing, Paul Mascon groaned and moved his head.

It couldn't have been morbid curiosity; Gail was too desperate to escape for that. It must have been an ingrained nursing instinct, a conditioned concern for anyone who needed help, that drew Gail to the injured man's side.

As Gail approached Paul Mascon, he released a long moan, turning on his side. The motion dropped him from his position on the windowsill, his body thumping to the floor with no more animation than if he were a lump of wet clay. Eyes glazed with pain, he looked up at Gail, choking, "Help me. Get me to a — doctor. I'm — hurt."

A widening spot of blood was soaking the gray suit in an area just below Paul Mascon's heart. He had either caught a stray bullet or someone in the yard below had seen and aimed at him. In a barely conscious observation, Gail saw that one of the windowpanes had been penetrated. A spiderweb of jagged lines radiated from a single clean bullet hole. The pane was not shattered. Neither were Paul Mascon's neat spectacles; they had been thrown to the floor by the impact of a bullet penetrating his body, but the glasses lay on the floor intact.

Torn between running and performing the duty to which she was sworn, Gail knelt down, wondering whether it was too late for first aid.

"Help me." Mr. Mascon gasped the words. "Telephone — downstairs."

"I'll get help," Gail promised. Considering the gun battle that was in progress, the statement had a ludicrous sound. Besides, if there was a phone available, why not call the police? An ambulance first. But why not the police? Provided, of course, that she could reach the telephone without being riddled by bullets. The gunfight below had reached an insane crescendo. "If I can get to the phone, I'll call for an ambulance," Gail said.

The man's eyes looked glazed, but a hint of alarm flashed in them. "No! No — get my doctor. Don't let — my family —" He gasped for air. Gail saw the thin lips move, contorting in an effort to say something else. There was a rattling sound from his throat, a telltale sound that Gail had learned to recognize. In the same instant, Paul Mascon's head sagged, rolling to a side. His eyes remained open, but no experienced nurse would have doubted that they were sightless.

For an interminable time Gail remained on her knees, staring at the dead man in shocked disbelief. It had been quiet downstairs for a few seconds. Now there was another shotgun report. Another. Gail got to her feet. She heard loud voices from the yard; someone yelling, "Leave 'im here. Let's *go!*"

A car whined as it was started up. Then the loud rumble of a motor being raced, a shriek of rubber against gravel, and the deafening sound of a vehicle racing away from the house were heard. Only one car. There had been at least three, Gail remembered. The other drivers were either dead, wounded, or . . .

Or on their way upstairs to see that their job was finished! Someone was clumping up the stairway. One of Mascon's men or one of the members of the lesser gang that had staged an insane attack. Whoever it was, he was moving with difficulty; the footsteps had a slow, measured tempo. Maybe he was hurt. Undoubtedly he carried a gun in his hands. Gail raced for the door.

There was no choice of directions. She turned to her right, running as quietly as possible down the corridor in an opposite direction from the staircase. At the end of the hall she miraculously found another flight of steps. Narrow. Dark. Laced with cobwebs and black as a bottomless pit. Gail felt her way down the steep incline, grateful for steps so rotten with age that they sank under her feet with a soft crunching sound rather than creaking.

She was breathing hard, every breath a prayer: *Don't let anyone hear me. Please . . . don't let anyone know I'm here!*

Gail shuddered, brushing a persistent cobweb from her face. Out of the darkness, she made out a glass-paneled door. She groped for a doorknob, found it with her left hand, turned the knob. The door groaned open, and she was in the weed-choked back yard of the house. Fear propelled her. She ran. When it was impossible to run any longer, when turning back revealed no lights from the house, only the faint illumination of a cloud-banked half moon, Gail stopped for breath. After that, avoiding rocks and jutting outgrowths of vegetation, she found herself, without wanting to be there, on a dirt road.

She had started to cry. Trudging along the side of a path that might return her to civilization, Gail found her strength being depleted by tears and a convulsive tremor of her shoulders. *They had been ready to murder her! Another few minutes and she would have lain as helpless as the small man who had ordered her death!*

Gail filled her lungs with air and then increased her speed. She was half-running again, desperate to reach the highway, when a flash of light threw her into a panic. *There was a car coming toward her!*

She had lost all sense of direction, not certain whether she was running away from the house or whether her route would return her to her starting point.

Twin beams of light caught her in their glare. They had seen her. Whoever was driving up the road had seen her, and now it was too late! Whether the approaching car contained members of the attacking gang or escaping remnants of Paul Mascon's "boys," she was finished. The syndicate's hoodlums seemed less of a menace now; it would have taken a drug-bolstered mob to stage that murderous raid on a more powerful gang. They would know her, too. They would have heard about her from Louis Fravel, from the waitress who had called herself "Mrs. Gibbs."

Gail covered her face with her hands and dived for the cover of a clump of palmettos. She felt the grating of sharp pebbles against the flesh of her knees. It was a minor pain, ignored in the overpowering grip of her terror.

Crouching behind the flimsy protective barrier, not daring to breathe, Gail felt her hopes sink as the approaching car slowed down. She opened her eyes, glancing toward the road to see that the car had stopped, its headlights illuminating a wide expanse of the roadside. Gail pressed her hands against her face, waiting for them to find her. There was no question that they would; the car had stopped only because she had been spotted.

There was the sound of a car door being opened, then another. Doors slammed. There were footsteps, the sound of people brushing against tall weeds, the rustling of palmettos being shoved aside to make way for someone drawing nearer to where she had huddled, lay pressed, face down against the humid soil, waiting — waiting for them to find her.

Someone near the road cried out, *"Is it Miss Arnold?"*

A voice yelled back in response. "I don't know. *Gail?* Gail, are you all right? Honey, it's me! Bruce. Gail, *where are you?"*

The footsteps had drawn closer to where she lay. There was no more reason to be afraid. It was only because she had grown accustomed to fear, because it seemed unbelievable that her ordeal had ended, that Gail remained motionless, caught in a rigor of terror.

She was still frozen in her frantic and hopeless position of hiding when Bruce Cranston's arms folded over her. Gail was only dimly conscious of the reassuringly familiar voice saying, "Thank God. Oh, Gail — I was so afraid! Thank God you're all right!"

Before she collapsed in his arms, she heard

Bruce call out, "She's here, officer. She doesn't seem to be hurt, but I want her rushed to a hospital. Can you come over here and give me a hand?"

Eleven

More than ten days elapsed before pieces of the puzzle began to fall in place. Most of the pieces followed Stella De Shiel's story of two rival organizations fighting for the exclusive rights to a sales territory. In the process, anyone who brushed against them was in danger. Stella had done more than that; she had become deeply enmeshed in both traps, inadvertently pulling Gail into the same terrifying snares.

"It's far from over," Bruce said. They were in the dispensary, waiting for the first of their afternoon appointments. "There's an investigation going on as to why the clinic didn't provide better security. The blame falls strictly on my shoulders."

"We were all lax," Gail argued. "I guess we've all been so involved with the victims that we didn't comprehend how vicious the people who victimized them were. It seemed too incredible."

"Fantastic amounts of money involved," Bruce reminded her. "Mascon, for instance, wasn't going to tolerate the slightest risk."

They were quiet for a few seconds, Gail remembering her ordeal at the hands of Paul Mascon and his gang. She had broken down completely when Bruce had swept her into his arms, carrying her to the police car and then to the clinic to be treated for shock. Gail had remained there, confined to a bed under Bruce's orders and under police guard, for three days. But she had gotten herself under control long enough before the police car raced off toward the city to tell the officers about the raging gang war that had made her escape possible. A radio dispatch had sent squad cars and ambulances to the site.

Apparently Bruce had been recalling the same scenes. "When you told me the police were already at your apartment, there was something so — hesitant about the way you talked, afterward I got suspicious. Then when you didn't answer the phone and the officers who had gotten your address from me didn't find you in, the search started. I was sick inside."

"You never did tell me how you knew where to look," Gail remembered.

"The customs people at the port had a hunch that there was a receiving station somewhere in the area. About a month ago, they'd stopped a contraband shipment of heroin; they were working with the narcotics division. Watching for similar merchandise, waiting for the same pick-up men at customs. They knew it was going to warehouses somewhere nearby; they'd gotten that far. Trouble was, Mascon kept shifting his base of operation. Easy for him, using a real-estate business as his cover. He'd use unoccupied houses or stores that were for sale. There'd be no occupant to trace. Or the phone would be installed under the name of an absentee owner. That old house would have been discovered sooner or later. But by that time Mascon would probably have moved his operation elsewhere. The truth is, when we started out — and by 'we' I mean every squad car available — all we had was a general suspected area." Bruce grinned at Gail fondly. "That and a prayer. Honey, until we saw you stumbling down the road — I was in a total panic."

Gail pressed her eyes shut for a moment. "I thought they'd caught up with me. If you want to know what total panic is . . ."

She had started to shake again, and Bruce crossed the room to take her in his arms. "Let's not talk about it anymore, darling. That part of it's behind us, thank God. My only problem is — I'm going to be a long time forgiving myself for what happened to Stella. The clinic board of directors is in a swivet. Afraid Mr. De Shiel will sue us for negligence. At the funeral he assured me that he just wants to — bury the past. But negligence could be proved in a court of law. I've been thinking — the decent thing for me to do would be — assume full responsibility and hand in my resignation."

Gail pushed herself back so that she could look into his eyes. "Bruce, you're not going to do anything of the kind! You're needed here. You're a doctor. You couldn't have been expected to be a crime expert — a detective. Even the police questioned Stella's story. It sounded so garbled! And she was so far gone on heroin. Bruce, *they* didn't begin to suspect Paul Mascon. How could *you* have taken that part of it seriously? And look at the way Fravel led me by the nose! You aren't going to quit. The only way you can make it up to Stella is by staying right here and helping people who've gotten hooked. You know perfectly well no one wants you to leave."

Bruce considered this for a few seconds. Then he said, "That's what Administration tells me. So, maybe it will all blow over. I just — maybe I'm looking for a form of expiation to square my conscience. A young woman warned us that someone was out to kill her. I let her die. It's as simple and as horrible as that."

"If you leave the clinic under pressure, every other doctor here, every nurse I know, will walk out with you." Gail, suddenly incensed, freed herself from Bruce's arms. "And if you leave this place out of some — twisted sense of guilt, when so many people here need you, I'll . . ."

Bruce had followed her across the dispensary, his hands reaching out to grip her forearms. "You'll what, honey?"

"I'll . . ." Gail let him take her back into his arms. "I guess I'll still love you, Bruce. I'll just be terribly disappointed. With most of the gang behind bars and the syndicate at least demoralized, maybe there'll be an increase in admissions. Junkies whose supply been cut off. You know what the percentage of 'cure' is."

145

Bruce held her close. "Maybe three percent. At Lexington about ninety-seven percent of the patients they released went back on the junk. Synanon's helping, but the odds are still heavy against the addict. Until somebody comes up with a better substitute than methadone, another drug that isn't addictive, I'd like to keep plugging along here. Sure, there's nothing I can do now for Stella, but . . ."

"There's a lot you can do for Pete Garvey." Gail looked at her watch. "He phoned to ask if he could come in early today. I scheduled him right after Hal. He's got a rehearsal at six thirty at the other end of town." Absently, she mentioned that Hal Benson, the first patient on their schedule, was late. There was always the possibility that he wouldn't come in, that they would never see him again. It wouldn't be the first time an appointment wasn't kept because an addict had gone back to "the real thing."

He wasn't showing up. Gail and Bruce filled the time with conversation, somehow returning to the subject uppermost in their minds. They couldn't avoid recalling the carnage that the ambulance attendants had found at the old house in which Gail nearly lost her life. Besides Paul Mascon there were two other members of the syndicate found dead. The mobster who had called himself "Officer Hart" was still on the critical list from bullet wounds in his chest. "Sergeant Russo" had died of gunshot wounds in an ambulance en route to a hospital.

And two members of the attacking gang had been arrested after applying for help at a New Orleans hospital. One was still there, barely holding his own. Then there had been the body of "Louis Fravel," mutilated by unspeakable tortures. Newspaper headlines had played up the story as a gangland slaying second only to Chicago's St. Valentine's day massacre many years ago.

They talked, too, about Paul Mascon's family, his friends and business associates, most of whom had been stunned by the news of his involvement in multimillion-dollar narcotics traffic.

"You wonder *why*," Gail observed. "He had a lucrative business. Nice family. He was respected by the community. Why would he have wanted more money? And such shoddy, murderous money, at that?"

Bruce couldn't answer that question. Neither could he explain why a clever attorney had chosen to become troubleshooter for a currently jailed nightclub operator and narcotics dealer named Virgil Corbett. Or why Fravel should have placed himself in a position where he either silenced a minor pusher named Stella De Shiel or faced death himself. The disbarred lawyer had been incredibly clever in gaining access to Stella's room. Why had he been stupid enough to try making a profit from the most ruthless criminal organization in existence? For that matter, why had a pretty, plumpish waitress placed herself in a spot where she could be ordered to kill a friend?

There was one consolation: The blonde who

had called herself "Mrs. Gibbs" was no longer in danger. Just short of being hooked, she was now a patient at the clinic. No one knew as yet why she and her supplier had been forced to make the attempt on Stella's life. Fortunately, no gangster who would have recognized her was still alive. Since Gail had returned to duty several days ago, she had been watching what promised to be a complete cure. For where therapy failed, a lesson in fear was doing the job.

Their dialogue had turned to Charlie De Shiel and how sorry they felt for him when the patient they had given up for lost came into the dispensary. He was a young man ("too young," Bruce had observed), disturbed because a flat tire had delayed him. As he exposed his arm for Bruce Cranston's needle, he said, "I was afraid maybe you wouldn't be here, I'm so late."

"I'll be here," Bruce told him. "Unless they throw me out bodily, I'll be around."

They were too busy after that for conversation. Later, when the patients who followed Pete Garvey had been dismissed, Gail filed away the charts. Debbie Farraday came into the dispensary to ask a question of the doctor. Bruce gave her the information she wanted, and the head nurse made a hasty exit.

Gail waited until Miss Farraday was out of earshot before she said, "Everyone's still waiting for her to say something about that ring on her finger. You've seen it, haven't you? That diamond's got to be bigger than a radish."

"My cousin Byron may be conservative," Bruce said. "But chintzy, he's not. Incidentally, he hasn't told me that he's engaged to 'The Sphinx.' Maybe he's letting her have the privilege of breaking the news."

"Well, she's not breaking it." Gail smiled, shaking her head. "She cornered me during my coffee break this morning. She said she had something wonderfully exciting to tell me. Naturally, I figured this is it. She's going to tell me she's marrying B. Cranston, D.D.S."

"Distinguished Dentist high up in Society." Bruce grinned. "But she didn't? What was the exciting news?"

"She found a new product that removes rust stains from toilet bowls."

"You're kidding."

"I'll swear it's true. Farraday *never* talks about anything that really matters to her."

They had walked to the door, and Bruce reached for the light switch. The dispensary was being closed for the night; the sudden semi-darkness was both practical and convenient. "Do you go around talking about things that really matter to you?"

Gail slid into his arms easily. The door remained closed as Bruce kissed her. It was a long, fervid kiss that left Gail breathless. "Did you want an answer to that question?" she asked.

"If you don't take too long. It's hard to kiss you when you're moving your lips."

"All right, ask anybody in this clinic. The orderlies, the lab technicians, the maids. Ask the maintenance man. Or the guy who cuts the lawn. If there are *any* people around who don't know you've asked me to marry you, they're on vacation. Bruce, I'm so happy, I've — I've told everybody. From Miss Farraday to Pete Garvey."

"Did you tell them *why* I proposed to you?"

"Because you love me."

"Because you're a naïve little kook who needs someone to keep her out of trouble." Bruce had been smiling, but now he was touchingly serious. His arms tightened, holding Gail so close to him that she had to gasp for breath. "Gail — honey, if anything had happened to you — if I had lost you, I —"

He wasn't able to finish the sentence. But there was another way to tell Gail how much he cared. It was a language they both understood.

For a long time, until someone was heard approaching the door, probably looking for a doctor who was invariably needed in several places at once, they communicated without the need for words.

We hope you have enjoyed this Large Print book. Other G.K. Hall & Co. or Chivers Press Large Print books are available at your library or directly from the publishers.

For more information about current and upcoming titles, please call or write, without obligation, to:

G.K. Hall & Co.
295 Kennedy Memorial Drive
Waterville, ME 04901 USA
Tel. (800) 223-1244
     (800) 223-6121

OR

Chivers Press Limited
Windsor Bridge Road
Bath BA2 3AX
England
Tel. (0225) 335336

All our Large Print titles are designed for easy reading, and all our books are made to last.